Innocent
PREY

A NOVEL

D. Whitesmith

Accent Books™ is an imprint of David C. Cook Publishing Co.
David C. Cook Publishing Co., Elgin, Illinois 60120
David C. Cook Publishing Co., Weston, Ontario
Nova Distribution Ltd., Newton Abbot, England

INNOCENT PREY
© 1993 D. Whitesmith

Cover design by Foster Design Associates
Interior Design by Glass House Graphics

First Printing, 1993
Printed in the United States of America
97 96 95 94 93 5 4 3 2 1

CIP/LC Number Applied for

To my husband—the sweetest man alive

Acknowledgements

Special thanks to: my cousin, Kim Lambert, for the medical information; the Ouray and Silverton Chambers of Commerce; my critique group: Debbie Bell, Kathy Cowan, Louise Harper, and Frances Shaw; and my heavenly Father for blessing me with this very special gift.

Note: To better serve the plot, some geographical liberties have been taken, including making Durango appear closer to Ouray than it actually is.

CHAPTER 1

"HELP! . . . HELP! . . ." A man's call drifted over the muffled roar of the Uncompaghre River.

Robert Hooper held his breath for a split second. A moment later, he dropped his rod and reel and scrambled down the bank toward the voice.

"HELP! HELP!" The calls came faster. The voice grew closer.

Robert fought through the few scrubby bushes lining the river, the smell of fresh water and fish filling his senses. His eyes strained against the glare of June sun on clear water and searched the narrow river's edge. He saw nothing.

Then something caught his attention on the river's other side. A stocky young man wearing a blue plaid shirt stood on the bank and stared intently at something heading downstream.

Robert's gaze followed the man's to a body slowly being sucked under by the current. It floated toward the river's center as it grew closer and closer to Robert on the north bank.

His heart skidded to a standstill. "I'm going in after him!"

"I can't swim!" the man yelled back, a new undertone of relief mixing with the urgency.

Robert ripped off his fishing boots and churned into the chilling water. It bubbled around him in white foam as the sharp rocks sent arrows of pain through his feet.

Robert struck out for the body. Was the person dead? Whether he was or not, Robert knew he would be soon. The man's submerged head pointed dangerously down-stream—where jagged rocks waited to pulverize anyone caught in their grip.

Panting, Robert struggled against the current. It tugged unmercifully at him. The muscles in his arms and shoulders ached as he clawed at the icy water. He felt as if he were running in a dream and not gaining any ground as the ominous, downstream roar beckoned its newest victim.

"You're getting closer. Hurry!" the other man called. He ran to keep up with Robert and the body.

Robert gritted his teeth until his jaw protested in pain. The current wouldn't win. He wouldn't let it. With one last burst of energy, Robert reached the man's side.

He turned the body over, securing an old man between his left arm and side. "Got him!" Robert yelled out in triumph to the young man, to the surrounding aspens, to himself. He strained to hear a cough or any sign of life. None came. Robert started his fight back to dry ground.

"Is he alive?" the man called.

"Can't tell," Robert said as water splashed into his mouth and trickled into his windpipe. He coughed, wishing it were the old man coughing instead of him. But Robert had felt more corpses than he cared to remember, and this man didn't feel any different—as cold as the trout in his fish basket.

Within minutes, Robert hovered over the victim, sprawled like a limp rag doll on the river's bank. Robert shivered, some from the water's chill, but mostly from fear at the sight of the elderly man's gray face and the rope-like lacerations on his neck.

"Is he alive?" the man called again.

Robert probed the man's wrinkled neck for a pulse. An unsteady rhythm fluttered against his finger, and Robert's hands shook with relief.

"Barely," he yelled back, recognizing the young man's fair good looks for the first time. He was Derek something or other, who owned one of the hotels in Ouray.

Robert prepared to do artificial respiration, but the old man coughed up a mouthful of water, then struggled to breathe with short, pathetic wheezes.

Robert glanced back to Derek. "Go get Sheriff Braxton, and tell him to meet me at Dr. Weston's." Taking a slow, deep breath, he fingered the abrasions on the old man's neck. "Looks like attempted murder," he mumbled to himself.

CHAPTER 2

D r. Toni Kirkpatrick plopped into the office chair and stared out the window at the bright day. She loved the way the blue mountains towered over Ouray. The rugged, snow-topped peaks reached toward the few fluffy gray clouds dotting the bright blue sky. The quiet beauty of Ouray, Colorado, outweighed Little Rock's hectic demands, and Toni didn't regret her move for one second.

Her stomach's rumble forced her to shift her attention to the most demanding desire of the moment, a juicy hamburger from Harry's Diner.

Just as she was about to take a big bite, the waiting room door burst open, banging against the wall. Toni looked up from her lunch.

A tall, wet man, wearing a straw cowboy hat, black western shirt, and blue jeans filled the doorway. He stomped toward her, water dripping from his sable brown hair.

Her backbone tensed ramrod stiff. She'd seen the kind of

panic which lurked in his near-black eyes too many times. Dismissing lunch as an unimportant casualty, Toni jumped up.

The man threw himself against the office counter, leaning heavily on it with his muscular arms. "Dr. Weston in?" he asked between gasps of air. The water from his hair created tiny puddles on the paper-cluttered desk.

Toni licked her lips. "No, but I'm a—"

"I've got an old man out in my truck. Found him in the river 'bout four miles from here. Get a gurney."

Within minutes, Toni and the cowboy wheeled the man into the exam room, careful not to jar him anymore than necessary.

"What did you do besides stabilize his spine?" Toni asked as she noted with admiration how neatly the two giant splints were taped to the back of the man's head and extended down his spine.

"That's it. He started breathing on his own."

"Has he regained consciousness?"

"No."

Leaning toward the old man, she pulled her golden-red hair out of her eyes and glanced at the cowboy. She needed to get this patient on oxygen. "Go—"

"You should have an oxygen tank around here somewhere. Go get it," he demanded. "I need to get him on it. The stranger ripped open the old man's shirt to expose a chest full of contusions which matched the lacerations on his neck.

This looked nasty. "I'm a—"

"Listen." The man leveled his determined, black gaze at her. "We don't have time for idle chat. Go get the oxygen. This man needs a doctor. See if you can find Dr. Weston, then call the hospital in Durango to send a chopper," he said, Texas style.

Toni gritted her teeth and went for the oxygen tank. She

9

didn't appreciate being ordered around like some first year med student. But right now this patient ranked higher than her pride. Besides, jeans and a worn-out T-shirt weren't exactly normal attire for an on-duty physician.

As the stranger listened to the man's lungs through a stethoscope, Toni rolled the green oxygen tank from the end of the oblong room. Wishing the new X-ray machine had already arrived, she made mental plans to check his vital signs, start two IVs, draw blood, and do a complete physical exam.

"He's definitely aspirated some water," the cowboy mumbled before grabbing the oxygen mask from her and placing it over the patient's mouth and nose.

As the stranger checked the old man's blood pressure, Toni took his slow, uneven pulse. The hospital needed to be called—quick. "Would you—"

"Ninety over forty-five," the stranger said. "Blood pressure's low. Need to get him on the heart monitor." He loosened the cuff from the patient's arm.

Toni picked up the cardiac leads lying near the monitor. "You go—"

"What *are* you doin'?" He reached over the patient and grabbed the leads. "I told you to go find Dr. Weston."

That did it! "*I'm* a doctor."

"Sure. And I'm Santa Claus. This is not playtime. You have no business in here, young woman. Go find Dr. Weston. Now!"

Toni's arms and legs shook with fury. She glared at him through narrowed eyes. "Look Mister—"

"Did I hear my name?" Phil Weston asked from the door.

Toni glanced at her uncle, swaggering into the room. Even at fifty, he looked more like a contender for the heavy-weight championship than a doctor. She exhaled in relief. Uncle Phil didn't know it, but he'd just stopped her from whacking this tall, arrogant man on the head with the nearest empty IV pole. The chauvinist!

She rushed for the door. Uncle Phil was her ticket away from him. "We've got what looks like attempted murder. Pressure's low. I'm going to call the hospital and Sheriff Braxton," she said. *Let him deal with that cocky man,* she thought and started out of the room.

"Wait," the cowboy said. "Somebody's already gettin' the sheriff."

Toni intercepted her Aunt Marge coming out of the office. Her doe brown eyes questioned Toni. "What's going on?"

"Poor old man almost drowned. And the abrasions on his neck and chest look like somebody tried to help him along. Looks like attempted murder."

"Oh my," Aunt Marge mumbled and hurried down the hall.

Having made her call to the hospital, Toni walked back through the exam room's doorway. The cowboy was taping IV tubes to the patient's arm. Uncle Phil had just finished drawing blood and was preparing to do a thorough exam.

Aunt Marge looked up from the head of the stretcher. "It's Jacob Tankersly, Toni" she said. "You met his daughter, Barbara, last week. I'm going to call her." She scurried toward the office.

Breathing a tiny prayer that the man would make it, Toni stood at the end of the gurney while Uncle Phil checked the patient's pupils and reflexes and listened to his heart. He was somebody's father, and probably somebody's grandfather. Toni's recent loss of her grandmother had left her with a special soft spot for older patients. She fingered her earlobe, toying with the ruby ear stud Grandma Weston had left her.

Toni moved to keep the man's neck stable while Dr. Weston and the stranger rolled the patient on his side for further examination. He moaned softly and seemed to be gaining consciousness.

11

The Texan told Uncle Phil everything about the rescue. Toni was pleased to know Derek Davidson had helped. He was one of the few people she'd met since her move to Ouray. Derek had been having trouble with muscle spasms in his lower back, and she'd prescribed a muscle relaxer. If he had helped save Mr. Tankersly, then he must be on the mend.

"Good thing you were there," Uncle Phil said when the cowboy finished. As they gently rolled Mr. Tankersly on his back, Phil Weston's kind gray eyes sparkled with admiration. "Sounds like you and Derek saved his life, Robert. I still say you should come to work as my assistant. We could use a paramedic around here."

Toni cringed. The very thought of working in the same office with him made her want to pack up her belongings and move right back to Little Rock. But that explained the great job he'd done on stabilizing the patient's spine. Robert was a paramedic. Well, he might be a paramedic, but he looked more like an outlaw from an old John Wayne western, day old stubble and all.

"I wish the X-ray machine were here," Dr. Weston said as he covered Mr. Tankersly with two blankets. Toni grabbed two more blankets from the metal cabinet in the corner of the room while Robert did another check on Mr. Tankersly's vital signs.

"Pulse is still unsteady," Robert mumbled.

"Pressure the same?" Dr. Weston asked.

"Yeah."

"I'm worried he won't make it," Dr. Weston mumbled. "Looks like somebody was playing for keeps."

Moving to the gurney's head, Toni wanted to get a better view of the rope-like red marks on Jacob's neck. She sympathized with his pain. Toni had seen more of these kinds of cases than she'd cared to in Little Rock, and she'd hoped Ouray would be free of such violence.

"He really took a beatin'," Robert mumbled, watching the heart monitor.

"I wonder why," Dr. Weston said. "He looks so defenseless."

Mr. Tankersly tugged weakly at the oxygen mask over his mouth and nose. His blue eyes fluttered open, and he stared straight ahead, terror fixing his gaze like a man who's seen the devil himself. His lips moved with undistinguishable whispers. Whatever he wanted to say, he looked desperate about it. Maybe he'd tell them who tried to kill him.

A cold, shaking hand grasped Toni's arm. The unseeing eyes of a few moments ago focused on her, pleading for understanding.

"Can you tell what he's sayin'?" Robert asked.

Toni leaned closer and removed his oxygen mask. "No." She pulled her hair away from her right ear and lowered her head to only inches above the barely moving lips. At first, a whispering breath fanned her ear. Then she sharpened her senses and concentrated on forming words out of the faint sounds. Finally, Toni understood him.

Her stomach knotted in a tight wad. Jerking up her head, she turned and stared at Uncle Phil.

"He said 'Murder number one.' "

As soon as Toni repeated the urgent message, the old man released his weak hold on her arm. His eyes fluttered shut, and his unsteady breathing pattern returned. With gentle, shaking hands, Toni replaced the oxygen mask.

Phil Weston's teeth clenched, making his square jaw appear even more square. "It's a crying shame," he mumbled. "And in Ouray . . . "

"What does it mean?" Robert mumbled. "Murder number one." He rubbed his mustache. "I'll be glad when Sheriff Braxton shows. We need to investigate the area for evidence. Maybe we can find the spot where he was dumped in the river."

"We?" Dr. Weston asked.

Robert squinted his eyes in confusion then smiled an almost boyish grin. "I guess I did say 'we.' Once a policeman, always a policeman."

Sheriff Braxton's voiced boomed from the doorway. "Derek here says you pulled ol' Jake from the river, Robert." The sheriff took off his hat and scrubbed his stocky fingers through his rough, auburn hair.

Toni smiled at Derek Davidson. "Sounds like you're going to be a hero," she mumbled.

Derek shrugged and grinned, his green eyes crinkling at the corners. "Robert's the hero. I just sounded the alarm. I didn't know if anyone was around, but I hoped someone would hear my yelling."

"Did you hear or see anything unusual before you spotted Mr. Tankersly?" Robert asked.

"Not a thing." Derek rubbed the back of his neck where his blond hair met his blue shirt collar. "And boy, was I shocked when he just came bobbing toward my fishing line."

"I've heard Derek's story. Now I need yours, Robert," Sheriff Braxton said.

Robert reported the details of what happened at the river, concluding with Jacob's recent words.

"And he said 'Murder number one?' What's that mean?" Sheriff Braxton asked.

No one had an answer.

Braxton leaned over to look at the marks on Mr. Tankersly's neck. Toni stepped out of his way, moving back to the end of the gurney. Tucking a strand of hair behind her ear, she couldn't stop the cold glance she threw in Robert's direction. His inky eyes stared back at her in speculation.

The man really had nerve. Coming into her clinic, pushing her around, and taking over like some cavalier. And the way he was staring at her—she'd seen that look

14

before. Coming from patients who were a tiny bit apprehensive to have such a young doctor, that look was under-
standable. But coming from him . . . forget it! Toni opened
her mouth, ready to quote the Hippocratic oath if that's
what it would take to prove to him that she really was a
doctor.

But the sound of helicopter blades chopping through the
air sliced through her oath plans.

In a matter of minutes, the helicopter's crew loaded
Jacob Tankersly into the chopper. From the waiting room
window, Toni watched the helicopter as Robert, Derek, and
Uncle Phil waved it off. The chopper hovered but a brief
second before gaining altitude and heading south toward
Durango.

The sheriff cleared his throat. "So all old Jake said was
'murder number one'?"

Toni gazed eye level at the sheriff. "That's all."

The clinic's door swung open. Toni watched Robert,
Derek, and Uncle Phil step into the clinic and head in her
direction. Robert towered over Derek and Uncle Phil, and
Toni wondered just how tall he was. She assessed his
height by hers. *I'm 5'11". He has to be 6'4" at least.*

Her scrutiny led her to a pair of dark eyes, which scrutinized her in return. Toni pressed her lips together, inhaled,
and glanced back at Sheriff Braxton. *Who cares how tall he
is.*

"Did you need me for anything else, Sheriff?"

"Don't think so. But I do need to talk to you, Derek. Is
there anybody who can confirm your story about this fishing trip?"

"Wait a minute," Derek muttered. "You don't think—"

"Course I don't," Sheriff Braxton said. "I just need to get
a clear picture, that's all."

Derek narrowed his eyes. "Right," he said, propping his
hands on his slim hips. "Ask Amelia Bingham, my recep-

15

tionist. She'll tell you I spend nearly every Monday of the summer fishing."

"Good, good. That's all I needed to hear. See, repetitive behavior is just as good of an alibi as an eyewitness sometimes."

Derek glanced uncertainly at Toni. She shrugged, somehow knowing that Derek could never be involved in murder. His soft green eyes were too kind.

She looked back at Robert's inky gaze. Now *those* eyes were a different story.

Toni touched Aunt Marge's arm. "I've got some errands to run, then I'm going home to finish my unpacking," she said. "The way today's going, I'll be here until midnight if I don't leave now."

Dr. Weston chuckled. "Looks like it. But we appreciate your filling in on your day off." He squeezed his wife's hand.

Marge tilted up her head, gave Phil a warm gaze, then turned her attention to Robert. "Today was our twenty-third wedding anniversary."

Robert's face broke into that boyish grin he'd exposed earlier. "Congratulations."

Toni scowled. Surely this wasn't the same person who'd come in here and taken over like he owned the place. She took a step toward the door. "See you later," she mumbled. The sooner she got away from Robert, the better. For the first time in her life, Toni had met someone whom she instantly disliked.

"Hey Doc?" Sheriff Braxton boomed.

Toni pivoted and looked at Sheriff Braxton. The surprised lift Robert gave one brow sent a glow of pleasure through her.

"The wife's doing fine after you told her to soak her feet in Epson salt. They're a lot better."

"Great." Toni smiled, then glanced at Derek. "I meant to ask you—how's your back?"

16

"I'm all cured."

"You *are* a doctor?" Robert asked in astonishment, apparently having heard enough to finally convince him. The man was insufferable.

"Exactly," Toni said frigidly, an instant replay of his "taking over" tactics filling her thoughts. Crossing her arms, she enjoyed the surge of heady triumph his shocked expression gave her. His widened eyes and obvious chagrin were almost worth all the aggravation.

Robert glanced over her blue jeans and faded red T-shirt, then looked back to her eyes. "But you can't be more than twenty-three years old."

Dr. Weston chuckled. Marge joined in. And Derek shook his head. "That's what I thought too, but—"

"I turned thirty in February," Toni said, leveling a gaze at Robert she hoped would freeze him.

"Well look at the way you're dressed." Robert tugged at his mustache. "How was I supposed to know?"

"I told you for starters." Her voice rose. "And if I remember correctly, you came out with a crack about Santa Claus." Toni's blood sizzled as she narrowed her eyes to thin slits.

Marge cleared her throat. "I seem to have missed something."

Flashing a bewildered glance to Marge, then Toni, Robert said, "I—"

"Well enough of this," Sheriff Braxton said, slapping Robert's back and glancing toward Derek. "I need you two boys to show me where you found ol' Jake, so I can try to find out what's goin' on here."

CHAPTER 3

Three hours later, Toni stepped onto her white porch. Clutching her keys in one hand and a bag of groceries in the other, she worked to get the house key between her thumb and index finger. With all her errands finished, Toni planned on spending the rest of the day unpacking.

Clenching her teeth, she huffed with impatience and propped the grocery bag on the black porch railing. Toni had been uptight ever since the scene at the clinic—the scene with Robert. Her shoulders were still as tense as they were when she had left the clinic. Using both hands Toni finally singled out the correct key.

" 'Bout time," she mumbled as if the key could hear her. Toni heaved the bag back into her arms.

Something fell off the porch railing and clattered to the wooden floor. Toni strained her eyes over the bag's edge and tried not to sneeze as it tickled her nose. Searching the

18

porch for what might have fallen, she noticed a white toy car rolling toward the middle of the porch. It slowly traveled across the old boards and squeaked to a stop.

Toni frowned. *Now where'd that come from?*

Maybe the Martin boy accidentally left it when they moved out before Toni bought the house. She narrowed her eyes in confusion. Wouldn't she have seen it before now?

Oh well. Toni stooped, picked up the car, and dropped it into her grocery bag. She'd call Heather Martin later and ask if Sam had missed it.

Within a few minutes, Toni unloaded her groceries and laid the car on her breakfast bar. But something she hadn't noticed earlier caught her attention. There were letters scrawled in red across the hood of the toy car. Narrowing her eyes, Toni tried to read the spidery words.

KILL YOU loomed out of the hair-like streaks of paint. Toni sucked in a deep breath.

Was this Sam's car? If it was, a nine-year-old boy didn't have any business writing KILL YOU on his toy cars. Somebody needed to tell Heather about this.

Toni planted the car beside her phone on the wicker end table. She'd call Sam's mom tonight. But right now, she had some more unpacking to finish. Maybe a few hours of hard labor would work off some of her aggravation with that rude cowboy—Robert.

Two hours later, Toni dropped to the floor and rummaged through some newspaper-wrapped pictures she had in a box. Robert hadn't been as easy to brush off as she'd thought he would be. Restless, she stood up and kicked an empty box. Her thoughts had fluctuated between poor Mr. Tankersly and Robert all afternoon. Now she was back to Robert.

"Rats," she muttered, walking into the big, old-fashioned kitchen. "Rats, rats, rats."

Sylvester howled from his favorite spot on the couch. Toni glanced at her feline buddy. "No, you can't have anything else to eat. You just ate an hour ago. You're like a bottomless pit."

Opening the refrigerator, Toni gathered the makings of a ham sandwich. Sylvester stretched and padded into the kitchen. "Cat," she said, "it's not that I want to think about Robert. I mean I really don't want to think about him. He's got to be the most arrogant man on the North American Continent."

Sylvester didn't care about Robert at this point. All he cared about was the contents of Toni's sandwich. He sniffed the air delicately. Toni slapped mayonnaise on her wheat bread and stopped to look out the kitchen window at the summer day slowly fading from existence. The mountain peaks sent long shadows over Ouray's serene beauty.

Shoving distracting thoughts to the back of her mind had gotten her through more than one exam in med school, but that trick wasn't working with Robert. "I'll just go slam a few tennis balls on the community courts, Cat—and pretend the ball is Robert's head."

She chuckled and continued to build her sandwich. Toni couldn't help but think how nicely he passed the tall test. She smashed the sandwich together with her flattened hand.

"So what! He passes the tall test." She looked down at Sylvester. "Why'd you have to bring that up?"

Sylvester yowled again, and Toni shook her head. "You're spoiled rotten." She laid a piece of ham on a saucer and put it under his nose. Toni scratched his black head then walked toward the couch with the sandwich and a bag of chips in one hand and a diet soda in the other.

All right, so Robert passed the tall test, but he also passed the arrogant test with a ten on a scale of one to ten.

No. Maybe a twenty. And the nice test? Forget it. He needed to read the Beatitudes.

Blessed are the meek.

*Ha! That man wouldn't know meek if it bit him on his
disgustingly perfect nose.*

Then why was he stuck in her thoughts?

"Who do I think I'm kidding?" she asked Sylvester a few
minutes later. "There's something so overpoweringly male
about that man. . . ."

Meowing, Sylvester peered up at the bird cage in the
room's corner.

"That's what I say. Who cares!"

With that decided, Toni popped the last of the sandwich
into her mouth and jumped up. She'd feed Tweety Bird,
then go slam those tennis—

A sharp pain stabbed her right knee. Toni shifted her
weight to the left, and fell back onto the couch.

"Oh no," she groaned. "What a day for old faithful to
erupt." Toni massaged her knee and fought the desire to
mentally lash out at the man who had done this to her. She
shut her eyes, knowing the forgiveness she'd finally experienced was too sweet to give way to the old bitterness. The
Lord had helped her let go of that bitterness, and she did
not want it back.

Sylvester jumped onto the end table, causing the little car
by the phone to fall onto the arm of the couch with a muffled thud.

"Hey Cat," Toni said, smiling, "you're messing up my collection." She pulled his furry, warm body onto her lap
before retrieving the car from between the cushion and the
side of the couch. Toni turned the cold, metal toy over in
her hand and rubbed her throbbing knee with the other
hand.

Like a streak of hot lightning on a sultry summer night,
the words singed through her mind. KILL YOU. And they

21

were on a white car. A *white* car. Her mouth went dry.

Toni wrapped her fingers around the toy, blotting out the blood-like words. The car's metal angles jabbed her palm, and she wanted to fling the tiny object across the room as if hurling away past memories.

With a deep, cleansing breath Toni willed her common sense to rule her wayward emotions. *No. It couldn't be. It's not connected.*

Relaxing her grip on the toy, she placed it beside the phone. The car was Sam's. It had to be. Her imagination had simply gone on a rampage.

CHAPTER 4

Robert killed his red truck's engine, looked at Toni's house, then glanced at his son, Bobby. He noticed Bobby's dark hair nearly grazed his yellow T-shirt's collar, and Robert made a mental note to get him to a barber soon.

"Okay. I'm only going to be in here about fifteen minutes. So don't get too involved with Jeff and his gerbils. Understand?"

Bobby shook his head and turned his dark brown gaze to his father. "But I still don't know why you have to give our pie to some ol' girl."

They slid out of the truck and slammed the doors.

"I told you," Robert said. "I was rude." He shrugged. "It's, well, it's like a peace offering. It's like when you and Jeff had that fight and he bought you a hamburger."

Bobby rolled his eyes. "But Jeff's not a *girl,*" he said, then headed across the street to Jeff Cornelius's house.

Robert grinned. Every female was a girl to Bobby, even grown women. And at this stage of his life, Bobby didn't see much use for any of them.

Robert made sure his son crossed the street safely, then started for Toni's door. He'd always heard that the way to a man's heart was through his stomach, and Robert hoped it worked the same for women too. Not that he wanted to get to Dr. Toni Kirkpatrick's heart. Being both father and mother to Bobby gave him too much to do without getting involved with a woman.

But she might more readily forgive him if he had a peace offering. Robert had acted like a jerk, and he knew it. This town was too small for him to be making enemies.

As he walked up the porch steps, he subconsciously straightened his shirt collar with his free hand and rubbed the side of his freshly shaven jaw. When Bobby got into the truck's cab a few minutes before, he had sniffed the air, coughed, and said, "You stink." Robert hoped he hadn't put on too much after-shave.

Balling his fist, he whacked the door then studied the pie. Was this such a good idea? *No!* a voice screamed inside. Trying to play mother to Bobby all these years must have somehow affected his brain. You didn't take things like cherry cheese pies to women. Not unless you were somebody's grandmother. And right now, that's about what he felt like.

Maybe she hadn't heard him knock. Maybe he'd hurry back to the truck, leave the pie there, come back to apologize, then exit.

Yeah. That'll be the right thing to do. And it'll even make Bobby happy, too. We can down the pie when we get home.

Robert's ostrich cowboy boots scuffed against the porch as he turned for the truck. But before he had a chance to take one step, the door scraped open. He stopped.

Well, dogies. Looks like I'll have to take the pie route after all.

24

Robert slowly turned to face Toni. Raising her brows in surprise, she glanced from his face, to the pie, then back to his face. Robert hoped he didn't look as dumb as he felt.

He cleared his throat. "Hello."

"Hello," she said. Leaning against the door frame, Toni crossed her arms, a wary yet curious slant to her mouth. And even though her eyes didn't look quite as cold as they had earlier today, they held a distinct chill all the same.

"I guess you're wonderin' what I'm doing here, after this afternoon and all," he drawled. Robert's chest tightened into a wad of nerves. He hadn't felt this awkward since high school.

"Well, yes, the thought *did* cross my mind." Her gaze went back to the pie.

With his left hand, Robert took off his black cowboy hat and held it to his side. "I came to apologize."

"Apologize?"

"Uh-huh. I'm afraid I didn't act too nice this afternoon. So I brought a peace offering." He shoved the pie toward her, hoping she'd take it so he could just get out of there.

Toni stared at it in disbelief. "Did you make it?" she asked, taking the pie from him.

"Uh-huh." He smiled at her and rubbed his right ear. "I have a nine-year-old son, so I have to do this sort of thing." *You sound like the president of the PTA.*

Robert crammed his hat back on, ready to leave before he did any more to embarrass himself. He'd never be able to face her again as it was. What would she call him? Grandma Robert?

Toni held the pie and regarded him with widened eyes. She appeared to be trying to make a decision, and Robert knew this was his best chance to exit. But for some reason he couldn't. The evening sun danced on her golden hair, urging Robert to admire the reddish highlights. Why hadn't he noticed how attractive she was at the clinic? All the

25

kitchen duty he'd put in must have blinded him or something.

Toni smiled hesitantly, and he thought his heart would fail him. That smile of hers was something else.

But her gray eyes took on the wariness again. And her smile diminished in a dawning awareness. Toni cleared her throat. "I . . . er . . . guess your . . . your . . . wife's glad you cook like this."

A flash of empty sorrow scurried through Robert's chest. But the realization of what her question suggested slowly banished the sorrow.

"No wife. Just me and the boy." His lips turned up despite himself.

"Oh really? Oh . . . I mean I'm sorry to hear . . ."

Consternation covered Toni's face, turning her into a floundering fifteen year old.

Robert's grin increased as she searched for the right words. Even though he knew nothing could ever develop between them but friendship, it did him good to know she'd embarrassed herself as much as he had. Now he could face her on the street.

She glanced down at the pie, inhaled, looked back at him, then smiled ruefully. "Would you like to come in for some coffee or something? We could share the pie." She held it up.

"No, I can't. I've got Bob—"

A loud crash, followed by a bird's screech and a cat's howl, stopped Robert in the middle of his decline.

"Oh no! The bird," she wailed. Shoving the pie into Robert's hands, Toni rushed into the living room.

He blinked at her back and tried to balance the cool, aluminum pan.

Through the half-open door, he heard her yell, "You crazy cat!" A cat growled. A bird shrieked. And something thudded.

What was going on in there? Cautiously, Robert peeped around the door and into the house.

Toni stood in the middle of an overstuffed, beige chair and tugged on a black cat hanging on the peach floral drapes with all fours. A turquoise parakeet sat at the top of the drapes, screaming in broken clucks. Toni's shoulder length hair looked as if she'd been through the fight of her life.

"One day, Cat . . ." she muttered under her breath.

Robert tried to suppress the laughter pushing against his throat. And he did manage to keep it down to a soft chuckle. Yet not so soft that Toni didn't hear it.

She turned and stared at him with a harassed expression on her face. "Don't just stand there and laugh. . . ." Gritting her teeth, Toni gave the feline one more swift tug, and he came free. "This is not funny," she said through a giggle of her own.

Clutching the furious, flat-eared cat, Toni walked toward Robert. "You better come in and close the door so Tweety Bird won't get out," she said as she tossed her feline boarder outside.

Closing the door behind him, Robert stepped into the living room. Maybe he'd visit for a minute or two. This didn't seem like the time to just up and leave. "Tweety Bird? The cat wouldn't be named Sylvester, would he?"

Toni smiled, exposing a row of nearly perfect teeth. "You guessed it." She took the pie from him. "Okay. So I'm a diehard Loony Tunes fan." She shrugged. "What can I say?"

Robert removed his hat and shook his head, smiling at her with unguarded indulgence. He couldn't help himself. "And you're sure you're thirty?"

Toni chuckled. "And a doctor, despite the way I'm dressed." She glanced down at her jeans and red T-shirt.

"I really am sorry 'bout that. Finding Mr. Tankersly 'n all . . . I wasn't exactly myself."

27

Toni waved her hand in dismissal. "Don't worry about it."

"Good. If you want the truth, it's still hard to believe you're thirty." Robert examined the youthful row of freckles dotting her nose. "I mean with those freckles and all." *Oh no! Why did I bring up her freckles!* "I—"

"Oh yeah, well, I inherited these from a long line of freckled noses." Toni chuckled self-consciously and rubbed the bridge of her nose.

Robert had to somehow make up for that stupid remark. "I think they're cute," he blurted, then groaned inwardly. "I mean. . . I didn't mean . . ."

"Would you like to sit down and have some pie?" Now it was her turn to smile indulgently.

He hesitated. Robert had come to make a clean apology and take an equally clean exit. And he'd hauled off and virtually flirted with the woman. He didn't want a friend who looked like her. He didn't need a friend who looked like her. And Robert knew he should make his escape.

But her gray eyes had taken on an uncertain, little girl glimmer as if she were afraid he'd say no.

"Sure, I'd like that," he heard himself say.

Toni grinned, the uncertainness leaving. She led the way to the kitchen and motioned to a backless bar stool. "Have a seat. Sorry about the mess. I'm not quite settled yet."

Robert lowered himself to the stool, placed his hat on the breakfast bar, and watched her dish up the pie. "Your uncle said you've only been here ten days. I guess that's why I haven't seen you 'round town."

Looking up from her task, Toni licked her index finger. "Yeah. I've kept a rather low profile. I've been busy unpacking."

"That's what he said."

Toni raised her brows. "What didn't he tell you?"

Robert turned up one corner of his mouth. "That's about it." *That is, unless you count the way he winked slyly when I*

28

asked your address. Robert had nearly told Dr. Phil Weston he could save his winks for a more eligible bachelor.

Avoiding the few boxes cluttering the kitchen floor, Toni placed a plate piled high with the cherry cream cheese confection before him. "This is my favorite dessert. One of the few I like coffee with. Want some?"

"I'd love some. Helps wash down this sticky stuff." His mind was playing tricks on him. Or had they really been in the kitchen—together—for years? A nostalgic déjà vu flooded his heart. Maybe Robert had missed female companionship more than he'd let himself believe.

" . . . do you mind?"

"I'm sorry," Robert pulled his gaze from midair. "I seemed to have drifted off. What did you say?"

"I only have instant. My coffee maker's still in a box somewhere. I'm not a big coffee drinker and haven't needed it until now."

"I don't mind instant. And I like it black."

"Figures," Toni muttered.

"What?"

"Nothing." Biting her bottom lip as if she were trying to stop a smile, Toni reached into the cabinet and pulled out two green mugs. "I called about Mr. Tankersly an hour ago. He's not doing too well." She filled the mugs with water and placed them in the microwave.

"Really?" Robert's heart clutched with concern.

Toni shook her head. " 'Fraid not. He stopped breathing and went into cardiac arrest on the flight over. They had to intubate him and put him on a ventilator. Now he's unconscious. In a coma. I was afraid that might happen. He's so old. His blood pressure was way too low. And with the water he aspirated, he'll probably develop pneumonia."

"How's the family taking it?"

The microwave bell rang, and Toni removed the mugs. "I don't know. Not too well, I imagine. I met his daughter,

Barbara, last week. Aunt Marge said there's only one son, and then Barbara's husband. No grandchildren." She stirred a teaspoon of instant coffee into each mug.

Robert stared into the kitchen. Images of Jacob Tankersly floating in the river blotted out the off-white cabinets. "I hope he makes it. I want to know who tried to kill him and why."

"Me too. It gives me the creeps to think there's somebody in this town who's a murderer. Who knows, I might even see the person and wave or something." She set the coffee down beside their pie and shivered.

"You're right. It's downright creepy. Just as creepy as what Sheriff Braxton and I found at the river." The aroma of fresh coffee blended with the smell of Toni's floral perfume.

She blinked in anticipation. "What?"

"Nothin'. We didn't find one thing. It's almost like it didn't happen. Whoever dumped him in the river took special pains to cover his tracks. Jacob Tankersly was a victim of cold-blooded, attempted murder. And the man responsible is probably running the streets of Ouray as we speak."

"How do you know it was a man?"

"The rope marks on his neck. They were too deep for a woman to have made. Normally women don't have that kind of strength, not unless they're weight lifters or something."

Toni took a bite of her pie, then sipped her coffee. Robert hesitated, but he wanted to ask her something he'd wondered on the way over here. Toni had acted as if she knew Derek Davidson, and she might be able to help him.

"You wouldn't happen to know whether or not Derek Davidson can swim, would you?"

Toni shook her head, a quizzical look in her eyes. "No, why?"

Robert inhaled. "Well, that's the reason he gave for not

going in after Mr. Tankersly. He said he can't swim."

"But would he have alerted you if he'd been involved?"

"Good point." Robert took a bite of the tangy pie. Even after all his years of police experience he still couldn't shake off the feeling which gripped him in cases like this. It wasn't necessarily fear—more of a haunting awareness of persons who could do something so evil.

When Robert considered what he'd gone through to become intimately aware of such wickedness, he wanted to stand on the highest mountain and scream until his lungs exploded. And at the same time, he cringed with shame—wishing he could wipe the memory of pair after pair of accusing eyes—wishing he could huddle in a hole deep in the earth's surface and never return.

But there was Bobby.

Robert blinked, and his coffee cup swam into focus. Inside he willed himself to calmness and glanced back at Toni. She was looking toward the large picture window in the front of the living room. Robert had been so lost in his thoughts, he'd almost forgotten he wasn't alone. And Toni looked as if she'd almost forgotten too. What was out that window which had so riveted her attention?

Robert glanced over his shoulder. Nothing appeared unusual from where he sat. The window offered a clear view of the asphalt road which stretched through the residential area. And only one white car slowly rolled past Toni's house.

Robert regarded Toni again. A glimpse of alarm clouded her eyes like a summer storm brewing on the horizon. Robert wondered what he'd missed out the window.

The parakeet tweeted for the first time since his near-miss with the cat.

"So are you enjoying the mountains?" Robert asked, his words woven with Tweety Bird's song.

Toni's eyes cleared, her lips tilting upward. "I love them.

31

I always told Uncle Phil and Aunt Marge I wanted to live here, now—"

Tweety Bird picked that exact moment to flutter from his perch on the drapes and come in for a zoom landing on Robert's shoulder. His slender feet scraped through Robert's shirt and tickled him.

"What's up doc?" the bird chimed in his gravelly parakeet voice. "What's up doc?"

Pleasant surprise warmed Robert's heart.

"Just like Bugs Bunny, huh?" Smiling mischievously, he coaxed the bird to sit on his finger.

Toni moaned. "I'm really not an overgrown adolescent. Honest."

"I'm not too sure." Robert chuckled, examining the green-blue parakeet gripping his index finger. "I didn't know parakeets could talk so well."

"If you get them young enough, you can teach them almost anything." Toni looked warily at the bird. "I think I should put him up."

"No, not yet. Can he say anything else?" Robert whistled, leaning toward the bird.

"Oh no," Toni moaned as the bird repeated the whistle.

"Robert's a hunk," Tweety said. He repeated the long wolf whistle. "Robert's a hunk."

Robert drew back from the bird in surprise. "How'd he know my name?"

Toni set her lips in a grim line and grabbed the bird. "He doesn't," she said as a half-blush barely touched her cheeks in a pinky-peach glow. "Robert's my brother. He thought it would be cute if Tweety spent the rest of his life saying that." She walked to the corner of the living room and placed the squawking bird in his cage.

"Hey. Don't put him up," Robert teased. "I kinda like him."

"I guess you do," she said, limping back to her bar stool.

"I think parakeet stew is on the menu for tomorrow. Care to join me?"

Laughter bubbled in Robert like a freshly opened soda. This was good for him, getting his mind off of . . . "Did you do something to your knee while you were chasing the cat?"

"Huh?" She looked at him blankly for a second. "Oh, my knee. Just an old war injury." The cloud of alarm reappeared in her eyes, and looking down, Toni raked her fork along the side of her plate in short, jittery strokes. But she lifted her gaze back to his and smiled.

"So, you're a soldier too? A doctor and a soldier?" he teased.

"Yeah. With a bird that doesn't know when to keep his mouth shut." The smile filled her eyes.

Robert returned it, enjoying the way her eyes sparkled with laughter. His heart was going to stop any minute. He knew it for sure. As their gaze lengthened, something resembling the fascination of a falling star flashed between them.

Biting her bottom lip, Toni broke the gaze, a hint of a blush on her cheeks.

Get a grip on yourself. Falling stars are for teenagers, not thirty-six-year-old men. Robert blinked, trying to settle his thoughts. He needed to get away from this woman while he still had a coherent thought left.

Someone knocked on the door, and Robert glanced at his watch. It was six thirty. Thirty minutes had passed since he told Bobby he'd only be fifteen. "That's probably Bobby. He was across the street checking out Jeff's baby gerbils." A tinge of guilt stirred Robert's midsection. How could he have forgotten his own son?

Toni answered the door. "Hello, is Robert Hooper here?" Sylvia Cornelius asked.

Robert groaned internally. This could get embarrassing.

33

Sylvia entered with Bobby at her side. She looked from Toni to Robert with heightened curiosity shimmering in her blue eyes. "I'm going to have to go to the gym now. It doesn't open until seven, but I've got to drop Jeff off for swimming lessons at Derek Davidson's hotel first. I think it's so nice of him to offer the town use of his pool."

"I lost track of time. Sorry." Robert stood, his heart lurching with what Sylvia had just said. Was Derek giving the swimming lessons?

"It's okay. I'll leave Jeff with you sometime." Sylvia tossed her long, brown-blond hair over her thick shoulders and waved as she hurried out.

Toni's gaze snapped to his, alarm clouding her eyes. So she'd caught what Sylvia said, too.

Shutting the door behind her, Toni smiled at Bobby. "Want a piece of pie?" she asked.

Bobby looked from Toni, to his father, then back to Toni. "No thanks," he said. "We don't have time. Dad promised to play catch with me tonight." Bobby's big, brown eyes held a betrayed accusation when he glanced back at his father. Robert sensed Bobby knew he'd forgotten him.

"That's right, champ," he said, crossing to his son. Robert had vowed a year ago that he'd never do anything to disturb Bobby's childhood again if he could help it. And he'd stand by that vow.

"I think we've got time to check into those swimming lessons before we head home, though. Your backstroke could stand some polishing."

"Cool," Bobby said, his eyes sparkling. Robert knew anything the ten-year-old Jeff was involved in Bobby thought was cool.

"Nice meeting you," Toni said. "You too, Bobby."

"Yeah," Bobby mumbled. Robert gave him a threatening poke in the side, and Bobby said, "Nice meetin' you too, I guess."

34

Shaking his head ruefully, Robert fumbled in his shirt pocket for one of his business cards. "I almost forgot. I'm the Ouray Handyman Service." He extended a white business card with raised black letters toward her. "If you ever need anything fixed, call me."

"I just might do that," Toni said, taking the card from him.

"And—um—I'll let you know what I find out about Derek," he muttered under his breath.

35

CHAPTER 5

T oni clicked the door shut behind Robert, then leaned against it for support until his pickup purred down the street.

Wow. Double Wow.

Pushing against the wooden door with her hands, Toni stumbled for the couch and sank into it. She picked up a newspaper and fanned her warm face. This was too much for one day.

Her insides churned like boiling water. Light-headed took on a new meaning for her. *Imagination. It has to be imagination.*

Toni Kirkpatrick—cool, scientific, level-headed—did not react to men, any man, like that. *Imagination.* She repeated, shutting her eyes. *It has to be imagination.* If it wasn't, then something magical just happened over that cherry cheese pie and coffee. Did Robert feel it?

She opened her eyes. Of course not.

She'd only reacted so because she was stressed out from trying to start her new job and unpack at the same time. And those white cars popping up everywhere hadn't helped her stress level either.

Of course Robert didn't feel it.

Forcing her pulse to settle and her mind to calm, Toni picked up the metal toy car lying beside her phone. In the back of her mind, a tiny doubt nagged at her assumption that this car belonged to Sam. Could that doubt be right? It was mighty strange that the same white car passed her house three times shortly after she found it.

A tremor of fear raised the hair on her arms. KILL YOU screamed up at her from the car's hood. Toni ran her thumb over the smooth, raised paint.

There was only one way to find out if this car belonged to Sam. She grabbed the phone book from the end table.

"Hello, Heather," Toni said when Sam's mother answered the phone. "This is Toni Kirkpatrick. How are you feeling?" The doctor in Toni couldn't call without checking on Heather's health. She was going to have a baby in four months. That's the reason the Martins had sold Toni their house and moved one street over. They'd soon be needing more space than their old, two bedroom home offered.

But Toni finally got down to the real reason she called. "I was wondering if Sam might have left one of his toy cars here when you moved. I found a little, white car on my porch and wondered if it might be his."

"No. I don't think so," Heather Martin said.

Toni bit her lip and studied the bird cage across the room.

"Sam loves trucks. He won't have·a car. He's got all kinds of trucks, though—big ones, little ones." She chuckled. "It might be nice to see an occasional car strewn across the living room floor, but he doesn't have any."

Toni's hand shook. "Thanks, that's all I wanted."

"Toni?"

Toni shut her eyes as the pulse in her middle finger palpated the car's bumper. "Yes," she said in a weak voice.

"Will you be at church this Sunday? Your uncle says you sang alto in the choir in Little Rock. We could use you."

Toni cleared her throat and swallowed in an effort to suppress the nausea spreading through her stomach and abdomen. "I plan on being there. I was called out to that car wreck on five-fifty yesterday and missed the service."

"That's what Marge said."

As much as Toni liked Heather Martin, she wasn't in the mood for an evening chat. Too much was going on. In a few seconds Toni managed to politely excuse herself from the conversation and hang up.

Toni stood up and limped around the living room. Her heartbeat slammed against her temples, and she knew a headache waited close at bay. This couldn't be happening. Would he do something so cruel? Wasn't what happened two years ago enough? It hadn't been her fault. Was he some kind of sick lunatic who preyed on other people's terror?

Sylvester yowled from the front porch, and Toni opened the door to let him in. Stooping, she picked him up and snuggled his soft, purring body. Toni cautiously looked up one side of the street and down the other. Was he watching her?

For the fourth time within the last hour a white car purred by. And old Mrs. Simms, Toni's next-door neighbor, waved at her from the driver's seat. Toni waved back and watched her pull into her driveway.

Shutting her eyes, Toni buried her face against Sylvester. Had the white cars she'd seen pass earlier been Mrs. Simms? The possibility released some of the throbbing in Toni's temples. Besides, if the person hadn't been Mrs. Simms, lots of people had white cars.

You have a white car, Kirkpatrick.

Okay. The cars earlier could have been anybody's. And the car she held in her hand, even though it wasn't Sam's, could belong to one of Sam's friends.

Maybe Mr. Tankersly's predicament had her overly sensitive. Shutting the door behind her, Toni hoped that was the case.

She wondered when Robert would let her know what he found out about Derek. Surely Derek Davidson hadn't lied about not being able to swim.

CHAPTER 6

The next morning Toni swept through the clinic, switching on lights as she went. She liked getting there a little earlier than everyone else. It gave her some quiet time. And since the clinic didn't officially open until seven-thirty, she had thirty minutes all to herself.

Toni went through the office, automatically straightening the desk chair. Entering the hall, she switched on the light and headed for the exam room to check the supply of gauze bandages. If she remembered correctly, they were low yesterday.

Yesterday. A day full of off-beat activities. Now, almost twenty-four hours later, Toni labeled it as an odd day. By the time she had gone to bed, Toni had convinced herself the white toy car and the cars passing her house weren't connected.

But Mr. Tankersly's problem was a different matter. She'd

expected Robert to call about Derek, but he hadn't. If he didn't let her know something by noon, Toni decided she'd find out herself.

Shivering, she thought of the evil presence of a murderer floating through Ouray's streets like an oppressing fog. Was it Derek?

Toni neared the exam room and wrinkled her nose. An offensive smell struck her and grew stronger with every step she took. If Toni didn't know any better, she'd think somebody had painted the whole clinic. A fresh paint odor permeated the air and invaded her nostrils.

Frowning, she clicked on the light to the exam room. Her eyes stretched open in painful horror. Her hands trembled. A cold sweat popped out all over her, concentrating on her upper lip. Toni gulped for air, but her lungs filled with paint fumes—paint fumes and panic.

She couldn't believe her eyes. It couldn't be there. Toni blinked, blinked, and blinked again. Yes. It was there.

A life-size dummy, dressed in a white lab coat and pants, wearing a blond wig, was pinned to the wall over the exam table. A monstrous knife, stabbing through her heart region, held her to the wall. And she hung there like an old Raggedy Ann with red spray paint glopped around the knife and staining the lab coat. The red paint trailed across her arm and marred the wall in a threat which convinced Toni the white cars were meant for her.

INTERFERERS DIE pulsed off the wall and branded Toni's brain like a cattleman's hot iron.

Toni's stomach threatened to unload the cheese pie she'd eaten for breakfast. Throwing a hand over her mouth, she whipped around and ran. Halfway up the hall, she bumped headlong into a tall, hard body.

It's him! her mind screamed. *He's come to finish you off!*

Survival instinct surged through her. She balled up her fist and slammed it against his lower abdomen. With a sur-

41

prised grunt and moan, the man doubled over. Toni ran around him, not seeing, not feeling, only fighting for her life. Turning, she planted her foot against his back side and sent him sprawling to the floor.

New groans coursed upward.

"Toni! My word, child, why are you beating up your uncle?" Aunt Marge cried from the end of the hall. "And what's that smell?"

Toni looked at her aunt in disbelief, waiting for her mind to register what she'd said. *Uncle Phil? Had she just hurt her uncle?*

Toni sagged against the wall, her knees shaking like a toddler's. She looked down at Uncle Phil, who propped himself up and leaned against the wall.

"Whatever I did, I'm sorry," he said.

Toni exhaled and shut her eyes, willing her stomach to stop squeezing against the cheese pie. "I . . . I'm sorry," she said through trembling lips. Toni inhaled, sucking in a new supply of paint odor. "But I thought you were . . . "

"Who?" the Westons asked together.

Toni gripped the wall with one hand and pointed toward the exam room with the other. "Go look. I'm calling the sheriff."

She groped her way up the hall and sank into the office chair. With her mind churning like a runaway freight train, she dialed the sheriff's number.

In a matter of minutes, Sheriff Braxton invaded the clinic. Toni answered all his questions and stood by while he examined the dummy and paint. Uncle Phil's and Aunt Marge's low voices, mixed with an occasional squeaking chair and shuffling papers, floated from the office.

" . . . and yesterday, I found a white toy car on my porch that says KILL YOU on it—in red. Then I saw a white car slowly pass the house several times. I wonder if all of this is connected to what happened two years ago." Toni wrapped her arms around her midsection and suppressed the urge to strangle whoever did this. *But that isn't part of forgiveness.* She swallowed, never wanting to be as bitter as she had been two years ago.

Sheriff Braxton glanced at Toni and back to the dummy. "I don't know, Doc. I'd come closer to believing this was tied in with ol' Jake's attempted murder than the past."

"But I didn't save Mr. Tankersly. Robert and Derek did."

"I know it. But whoever did it might not see things that way."

"Well how do you explain the cars then?" Toni asked, raising her hands.

Sheriff Braxton shrugged. "The toy could belong to half the boys in Ouray. And the other half of Ouray drive white cars. I know you're spooked. You've got every right to be. But it's probably just a coincidence."

Toni pondered whether or not she should tell Sheriff Braxton about Derek Davidson's possible lie. Crossing her arms, she decided against it. Toni didn't want to throw a shadow on Derek if he'd been telling the truth about not being able to swim.

"What's happened?" a deep, male voice questioned from the door.

An unusual surge of relief flooded Toni. The sight of Robert Hooper somehow calmed her nerves and eased the knot in her stomach. The man radiated a strength which— senseless as it might seem—made Toni believe that she was safe.

"I was passing by and saw your car, Sheriff, and thought I'd see what was going on." Robert's eyes shone with warm concern as he looked at the dummy, then at Toni. He tugged on the collar of his faded denim shirt.

Toni stared at the dummy as the two men discussed her dilemma. Her toes curled against the confining barriers of her tan, leather shoes. And her nails ate into her hands just as that little car had pressed into her palm yesterday. Was Sheriff Braxton right? Were the cars mere coincidences? Something told her they weren't. But why was this happening to her?

"Can you go home and get that car, Doc?" Sheriff Braxton asked.

Toni blinked. "I thought you said it was a coincidence."

"Probably is. But Robert thinks with everything else that's happened, it won't hurt for me to take a look at it anyway. I think he's right."

"Okay. I'll run home and get it. Won't take but a few minutes."

"I'll follow you out. We need to talk," Robert said.

"Hold on, there," Sheriff Braxton said, placing a hand on Robert's arm.

Robert turned to face the sheriff.

"I want you to think real hard and see if you can come up with anything new—maybe something you forgot to tell me—about what happened at the river yesterday."

Toni inhaled sharply and watched Robert. She wondered if he would mention the question about Derek's swimming.

"All right," Robert said slowly.

Sheriff Braxton cleared his throat and lowered his voice. "The reason is that I checked with Derek's receptionist on his fishing. She said sure enough that he does fish every Monday of the summer. But he told her he was going to Molas Lake yesterday, not the Uncompaghre River. I talked to him about it. He said he'd changed his mind after leaving the hotel. That's all fine and well and very possible. I know I've changed my mind about fishing holes before, but I didn't like the way his eyes shifted. I don't know . . . something's bugging me about this."

"How do you know *I* didn't do it?" Robert asked, narrowing his eyes as if he were challenging the sheriff.

"I don't. But you don't even know Jake."

"How do you know I don't know him?"

"I asked his daughter." He scrutinized Robert as if he were trying to get inside his thoughts.

"So? I'm sure there are things his daughter doesn't know about him."

"I'm sure you're right. But I also know I ain't spent forty years in this business without knowing how to read people."

"Did Derek know him?" Toni asked.

"Sure did. Mr. Tankersly and three or four of his buddies met every day for lunch and dominoes at Derek's hotel restaurant. Derek had a special corner set up for them."

"But that doesn't give him a motive," Robert said.

"I know," Sheriff Braxton said, a frustrated gleam in his eyes.

"And why would Derek alert Robert to save Mr. Tankersly if he was the one who tried to kill him?" Toni asked.

"I've thought of that too. Only answer I can come up with is he might've thought the old man was dead, and—"

"And it would make him look mighty good if he acted like he wanted Mr. Tankersly to be rescued," Robert said.

"Right," Sheriff Braxton said.

Robert walked toward the door. "I'll see if I can come up with anything new."

"I'll be back in a few minutes, Sheriff," Toni said and followed Robert outside.

"So what did you find out?" she asked as soon as the clinic door shut. The bright morning sun warmed the crisp mountain air, and Toni squinted against its rays as she looked up at Robert. Having to actually tilt her head back to look into a man's eyes was a rare—and very nice—experience.

"The swimming lessons are being given by a teenage boy in town who volunteered to do it for the summer just for fun but didn't have a pool to do it in. Derek offered the hotel's heated pool as a gesture to the community." Robert shrugged. "I enrolled Bobby."

"But we still don't know whether or not Derek can swim."

"I know. That's why I didn't say anything. Derek seems like a really nice guy. I'd hate to make him look suspicious if he was telling the truth."

"I didn't say anything for the same reason."

"Did you notice . . . nah."

"What?"

Robert shoved his hands into his jeans pockets. "Did you notice what Sheriff Braxton said when he first came to the clinic yesterday?"

Toni tried to recall all that had happened. "No . . . there was so much going on."

"He said, 'Derek says you pulled ol' Jake from the river, Robert.' What I want to know is, how'd Derek know it was Jake?"

Toni's eyes widened. "I hadn't thought about that."

"I mean, when I saw him, he was face-down, and the river was pullin' him under. I didn't get a good look at his face till I turned him over on the bank."

"Is the river narrow enough for Derek to have recognized Mr. Tankersly from the other side?"

Robert shrugged. "Could've been. I recognized Derek from across the river. That's a good point. I guess I'm startin' to grab for straws, and I shouldn't." He glanced away. "I don't agree with assuming someone's guilty until proven innocent. And as far as I'm concerned, we don't have enough to go on with Derek right now. He's still innocent." He stared toward the white-peaked mountains, which looked nearly close enough to touch. A stony glint turned his eyes into hard onyx; his thoughts seemed to leave her and travel to another time and place.

Toni checked her watch, her fingers still trembling from the ordeal she'd just gone through. "I'm going to have to run. I've got a patient in fifteen."

"Right." Robert touched her arm, the coldness in his eyes melting. "Now you take care of yourself, you hear? I don't like this business." He hesitated for a minute, then went on. "Feel like telling me what the deal is with the car?"

Toni shook her head. "I'd really rather not talk about it right now."

"Oh," Robert said awkwardly.

"It's not you." Toni laid a hand on his forearm, her fingers tingling with the feel of muscles under taut skin. "It's just that I don't think I can talk about it right now. Not with all that's happened."

Robert covered her hand with his. "I understand," he mumbled as if he really did.

Toni swallowed, her heart skipping a beat. "Thanks."

"Just be careful."

"I will."

By lunch Toni had seen four patients and one little boy's collie, which had a broken leg. And between patients, Toni found herself thinking about Robert. She wouldn't give herself the freedom to speculate on anything else for the sake of her nerves.

But there were lots of things she wanted to learn about Robert—like what happened to his wife for starters. Was she dead? If Uncle Phil stayed true to character, he'd have all the information Toni wanted, and probably some things she wouldn't even think to ask.

Easing into the office chair, Toni rolled up to the desk and pulled her mayonnaise, onion, and peanut butter sandwich from its brown paper bag. After a morning of Aunt Marge and Uncle Phil hugging her or patting her on the back with love and reassurance every time they got a chance, Toni wanted to avoid talking about the dummy or the car.

She looked across the desk at Uncle Phil who was in the process of devouring a juicy hamburger. The smell of cheese on beef tantalized her, and Toni suppressed the urge to take the hamburger away from him.

She took a bite of her sandwich. Not wanting to cause undue speculation about her and Robert, Toni teetered on the brink of asking Uncle Phil about Robert's wife. Uncle Phil, matchmaker of Ouray County, would take even the slightest interest and run with it.

Dr. Weston looked at her with penetrating eyes and massaged his midsection. "I guess that's one of your famous onion, mayonnaise, and peanut butter sandwiches?"

Toni smiled. "Yeah. And don't start."

"I won't start. But it's disgusting."

"I thought you said you weren't going to start."

"Okay, I won't. So what do you think of Robert?" he asked, changing the subject with record speed.

"What?" Toni groaned to herself. Uncle Phil was one step ahead of her.

"Robert. What—"

"How's your abdomen?" Toni glanced across the office at Aunt Marge, bent over a mound of gauze bandages. Was that a tiny smile on her lips?

Uncle Phil grinned. "I'm going to live. You throw a pretty good punch, kid." He grimaced in sore appreciation.

"And what about your . . . gluteus maximus?"

He chuckled and shook his head. "What do you think of Robert?"

"Why do I feel like I'm being set up?"

"Well, he did visit you last night. And every time you passed the exam room while he was repainting the wall this morning, he stopped and watched you go by."

"He didn't and you know it." Toni wished she could bail out of this conversation.

48

"But you can't argue that he didn't go to your house last night."

"Yes. He did come over last night. But that doesn't mean anything." *I hope it means something.*

"Of course it doesn't mean anything. But I just wondered how it went." He placed a yellow pencil behind his left ear and rubbed the golden-gray hair above it in a gesture Toni had seen many times over the years. Uncle Phil, in his non-chalant way, was conducting his own investigation, and Toni was the subject.

"What he's trying to say, Toni, is he wants all the gory details," Aunt Marge said.

Toni smiled fondly toward her aunt. Sometimes she wondered how such a thin woman kept up the pace as office nurse and secretary. Looking back at her burly uncle, Toni studied him over a stray piece of onion sticking out of the top of her sandwich. Since they were on the subject, she might as well find out all she could.

Feeling as if she were hanging herself, Toni switched her gaze to her sandwich. "What do you know about him?" she asked in the most casual voice she could conjure up.

"Born November twelfth. One brother, named Michael. Both parents live in Dallas—been married forty-one years. Wife killed in a car wreck seven years ago—named Pam. One son—Bobby—age nine. Ex-paramedic and policeman. Born and raised in Dallas, Texas. Tall, dark, handsome, Christian, and did you notice he passes the tall test?"

Marge chuckled.

Toni groaned and rolled her eyes upward. "Now I know I'm being set up. You missed your calling, uncle of mine. You should've been a professional busybody."

"You didn't answer my question," Dr. Weston said. "He passes the tall test—did you notice?" He sipped his tea, his eyes twinkling over the glass's edge.

Aunt Marge headed down the hall, her arms full of gauze

49

bandages. Toni eyed the handful of bandages left lying on the counter. Wanting to escape Uncle Phil's questions, she knew only one way to do it. Run!

Shoving the last few bites of sandwich into the brown bag lying on the desk, Toni took a sip of her diet soda and rolled her squeaky chair away from the desk. "You know that tall test was high school stuff," she mumbled, walking toward the bandages.

"It might've been. But you were serious. To my knowledge you've never gone out with anybody since then unless he was a good three inches taller than you. And just guessing, I'd say Robert is at least four, maybe five inches taller than you. Did you notice?"

Toni loaded her arms with the bandages. "Well, if you'd seen how I towered over Tommy Randolph the whole evening, you wouldn't blame me for making sure—"

"Are you going to answer my question?" Mischief danced in his eyes.

Fear of being found out edged Toni toward the door. She knew if she admitted to noticing *anything* about Robert, Uncle Phil would enlist the National Guard if that's what it took to get Robert and her together. "I'm going to take these to the exam room." Toni held up the bandages and tried not to break into a tell-all smile.

Uncle Phil winked slyly. "I thought you noticed." Leaning forward he whispered, "I won't mention it to anybody. Not even your aunt." His eyes teased her.

Toni felt like a trapped rabbit. And the smile pushing against her straight lips only reflected a glimmer of the internal smile which broke out every time she thought of Robert. "Sure. You'll probably take out an ad in tomorrow's paper. 'TOP STORY: ROBERT HOOPER PASSES THE TALL TEST.' " The smile won.

Mock horror rounded his eyes. "Me? Well, I wouldn't—"

The phone's ring cut through their conversation. Uncle

50

Phil turned to answer it, and Toni darted down the hall. She forced herself to walk through the exam room's doorway. And her throat tightened when she saw the fresh, white paint which blotted out the blood-like message. The odor filled the clinic, but remained most intense in this area.

Aunt Marge looked up from the metal cabinet in the corner where she neatly stacked gauze bandages. Her light expression from a few moments ago gave way to apprehension. "I wonder who did it?"

A dark foreboding filled Toni. "I hope he's not going to go through with it." She rubbed her chest and swallowed.

"I know you need your space and all that, dear, but have you thought about staying with us for a while?"

"I've thought about getting a dog. But I don't like to run. You know that. And besides, what would I do with Tweety Bird? Uncle Phil would sneeze himself senseless the first night."

"That's what your uncle said you'd say. If you just had a husband. . . ." Aunt Marge trailed off thoughtfully. She looked at Toni apologetically. "Sorry. I'm starting to sound like Phil."

"It's all right. I know you're just worried. I'm worried, too."

CHAPTER 7

The next evening Toni drove to Durango after work, much to the consternation of her uncle and aunt. She needed to get away from Ouray. Toni had to have some space. And going to check on Mr. Tankersly gave her the perfect chance.

After her hospital visit, she planned a shopping trip. She hoped it would lift her spirits. And besides, Toni wanted to look more—more presentable the next time she saw Robert Hooper. He made her more aware of her appearance than anyone else ever had. And that awareness told her she could use a major overhaul—makeup and all.

Toni drove into the hospital parking lot and stepped from her car. She smoothed the camel dress pants from two years ago, then fidgeted with her grandmother's three carat diamond pendant resting against her old beige, tailored shirt. Shopping—a must.

Sighing, she headed for the hospital entrance. When

she'd called and spoken with the ICU nurse earlier today, Mr. Tankersly's report was the same. Still in a coma, no response.

"Toni?" a man shouted from behind her. "Hey Toni!"

Toni smiled before she turned around. "Hello," she called to Robert.

Robert closed the distance between them and returned her smile. "What's the rush?"

Hit by his overpowering presence, she hesitated. Had his shoulders been that broad yesterday morning? Or did the gray sports jacket he wore with his blue jeans make those shoulders look like they'd grown six inches? Now Toni couldn't remember what he'd asked. "What?"

"What's the rush? I began to wonder if I was going to catch up with you."

"Catch up with me?"

Robert opened the glass door, and she preceded him through it. "Yes," he said hesitantly as an oops-I've-said-too-much look covered his face, and wrinkled his brow.

"Did Uncle Phil send you as my watchdog?" Toni demanded as they approached the elevators.

"If that means he asked me to drive over and keep an eye on you, I guess so." He followed Toni onto the elevator. "I stopped by the clinic to see if—well—to make sure you were still all right. That dummy thing bothered me. It bothered your uncle and aunt, too."

"So they begged you to follow me?"

One side of Robert's mouth lifted. "They didn't have to *beg* me."

Toni tucked a strand of hair behind her ear and wished her heart wouldn't stop every time he smiled like that. "Where's Bobby?" she asked.

"The church is havin' a double feature video night for the children—*Old Yeller* and somethin' else."

The elevator doors swished open, and Robert followed

Toni out. "Do you mind that I came?" His anxious gaze searched hers.

Toni blinked at the warm rush in her midsection. "No." When she told Aunt Marge she'd thought about getting a dog, Robert wasn't the breed she had in mind. But he'd do.

They arrived in front of a door marked "Intensive Care Unit," and Toni glanced at him. "They won't let you in here. You can go into the waiting room until I get back." She pointed toward a large room which opened onto the hall.

A middle-aged woman slumped in one of the chairs. Her eyes, swollen and red, glistened with tears, and she dabbed her nose with a tissue. Three men accompanied her. One stared out the window that looked onto the parking lot. Another stood behind the woman with his hands resting on her shoulders. And the third man sitting in one of the chairs resembled the man standing behind the woman.

"Is that his family?" Robert asked.

"Yes. That's his daughter. I haven't met his son or Barbara's husband. They must be the ones standing. And I don't know who the man sitting down is."

Robert headed in their direction, and Toni pushed against the ICU door, enjoying the faint trail of sandalwood Robert left behind. The door shut behind her with a soft sigh.

The ICU ward smelled of alcohol and clean sheets. The RN on duty ushered Toni into Mr. Tankersly's room.

"Any response since I talked to you?" Toni asked from the end of Mr. Tankersly's bed.

The dark-haired man frowned, forming a crease between his brows. "No response. But something strange happened about two hours ago."

An alarm bell sounded in Toni's mind. Too many strange things were happening. "Oh, really? What?" she asked.

"The maid came in to empty the trash cans and found his ventilator unplugged."

Toni glanced toward the old, gray-haired man swathed in

white sheets and then to the RN. The hair on the back of her neck prickled. "He could have died."

"I know. I replugged it and called the doctor immediately. But Mr. Tankersly was breathing on his own, and I don't know how long it had been disconnected."

Toni searched for a logical explanation, hoping this didn't fall into the scheme of some sick man's mind. "Do you think the maid may have accidentally unplugged it and was afraid to tell you?"

"I thought about that. I don't know. The hospital employees and, of course, his family are the only people who have been in here today. And I don't think—"

"All four of them have been in?"

"There's five of them, isn't there?"

"Five?"

"Yeah. A daughter, a son, a son-in-law, the son-in-law's brother, and then the grandson."

Toni's heart thudded. Aunt Marge told her yesterday that Jacob Tankersly didn't have any grandchildren. Doug never married. Barbara and Frank didn't have any children. "What did the grandson look like?"

The RN assessed Toni's height. "'Bout your height. Blond hair, light green eyes, clean cut, very nice."

"Did you get his name?"

"No. You—you don't think—"

"Mr. Tankersly doesn't have a grandson."

The man's brown eyes widened in alarm.

Had he just described Derek? "Mr. Tankersly could have died," she mumbled.

"That's what Dr. Lyeson said. But he was breathing on his own, so Dr. Lyeson's going to take him off the ventilator again for a little while tomorrow and watch him closely to see how he does."

"I'd recommend not letting the blond man back in here. He isn't family."

55

"I won't."

"Good."

"If you need me, let me know," the RN said, stepping toward the nurses' desk.

Toni turned her attention to Mr. Tankersly. The wires and tubes attached to his body connected to a variety of pumps, monitors, and dripping bottles. The hiss of modern technology added to the pathetic man's silent appeal.

Toni gritted her teeth. *Whoever did this should be here. Not this old man.* Her chest felt as if it were caving in with frustration. Was the same man to blame for her pain? Sheriff Braxton didn't seem to think he was. Toni hoped her past wasn't coming back to haunt her, but a foreboding voice told her otherwise.

And she didn't know if she had the strength to leave forgiven the old hurts. Forgiving someone for what happened in the past was one thing. Maintaining that forgiveness through another attempt on her life was something else.

Moving to Mr. Tankersly's head, Toni gripped the cold, metal siderail and leaned over him. His sunken eyes looked like two holes in his colorless face. And the white sheets accented the bruises on his neck and temples, making them appear more black than blue.

"You've got to regain consciousness, Mr. Tankersly," Toni whispered. "We've got to find out who's responsible." Toni hoped this time the criminal wouldn't go free.

"Lord, touch him," she breathed. Toni wished she could transfer some of her youthful strength to him.

Ventilators didn't unplug themselves. And she wondered who was responsible. Was Derek the man the RN had just described?

Toni walked back through the cold ICU ward and into the hall, her chest still tight with frustration.

Only a few feet stretched between the ICU door and the waiting room where Robert sat in silence with the family.

Toni walked up beside him and cleared her throat.

"You're back," Robert said in a relieved voice as he stood.

Toni nodded and glanced at the room's other four occupants. Could one of these people be capable of pulling the cord on a ventilator? Her gaze went to the man standing at the window. His gray shirt complimented his iron-gray hair and sky blue eyes which smacked of Mr. Tankersly's looks. Could a son do that to his father? Or what about the granite-eyed man in the navy tweed jacket standing behind Barbara? Or the man wearing the blue sweater who sat in the chair? He resembled the granite-eyed man, so they must be brothers. What about Barbara?

Toni hoped Barbara wasn't involved. Her mousy brunette hair looked just as haggard and tired as her eyes. Besides, Robert said the marks around Jacob's neck were too deep to be made by a woman. And Barbara didn't look like a weight lifter.

"I'm really sorry about your father," Toni said. "There are a lot of people praying he'll make it, including me."

"Thanks," Barbara whispered. Her eyes held a pathetic, silent plea which tore at Toni's heart.

"You're Dr. Weston's niece, ain't you?" Barbara's husband accused. Toni glanced up to meet a granite-like gaze. Chills raced up and down her arms as his long face twitched. "Yes."

"You're the one who got ran over a couple of years ago," he sneered.

The shock of what he said hit Toni in the face like a two-by-four. She relived the agony of crunching bone smashed between asphalt and rubber. The toy car flashed to her mind, then the dummy. Toni took a deep breath in an effort to regain her composure. Her face grew cold. She must have gone pale because Robert laid his hand on her shoulder.

"Yes, I'm the one someone ran over. How did you know?"

He shrugged and looked away, rubbing his brown hair as if he'd lost interest. "It was big news. Everybody knew about it."

Barbara's brother stepped forward. "I'm Doug. Doug Tankersly." He extended a hand in Toni's direction.

"He owns the hardware store in town," Robert said.

Toni shook Doug's hand, glad for the diversion. With Robert's reassuring hand on her shoulder, Toni's mind and emotions began to right themselves.

Doug continued, "And this is Frank Jones." He pointed toward the granite-eyed man.

Frank didn't extend his hand to Toni, and she was glad. He gave her the creeps. She stopped a developing shudder.

"And this is Frank's brother, Gordon."

Toni shook Gordon's hand.

"Nice to meet you," he said softly.

Doug's clear, blue eyes assessed her. "We're glad you came to see Dad." He didn't sound very glad.

Robert inhaled. "Well, it was nice meetin' y'all," he said in an overly polite voice. "Let's get out of here," he whispered.

Toni didn't need much persuasion. Something about Frank Jones made her want to run as fast as she could in the opposite direction. No wonder Barbara looked so trampled.

On an impulse, Toni bent and hugged Barbara. "Please let me know if I can help you," she whispered.

Barbara's arms circled Toni's neck in seeming desperation. A soft sob escaped her, and Toni thought her heart would break. Something told her there was much more to this than the surface showed.

Barbara finally released her hold. Toni pulled away, patting Barbara's shoulder and throwing one last look at

Frank's sullen face before she started down the hall at Robert's side.

"If you ask me, Frank is *Twilight Zone* material," Robert mumbled under his breath.

"I second that motion," Toni whispered, cringing. "How could two brothers look so much alike yet be so different? Gordon seemed nice."

"I know. He was the only one who really bothered to talk to me while you were in to see Mr. Tankersly." They neared the elevators. "How was Mr. Tankersly anyway?"

"Doing well considering somebody unplugged his ventilator."

"Unplugged his ventilator?" As they stopped in front of the elevators, Robert's eyes revealed shocked dismay. He pressed the down button, and the doors swished open.

"My reaction exactly. The nurse said the maid found it unplugged, and he didn't have a clue who did it. He seems to think the maid was responsible and was afraid to tell him."

"Who all's been in there today?"

The doors reopened, and Toni preceded Robert into the foyer. "Frank, Doug, Barbara, Gordon, hospital employees— including the maid—and somebody saying he was Mr. Tankersly's grandson. The only problem with that is Mr. Tankersly doesn't have a grandson."

Robert stopped just as they stepped outside. "Whoa. Did the RN get a name? A description?"

"No name. But he said the young man was about my height, blond hair, green eyes, clean cut, and very nice. Sound familiar?"

Robert peered out over the parked cars. "I was going to tell you Barbara mentioned that Derek came to visit about two hours ago. Sounds like his description."

"And it was about two hours ago that the maid found the ventilator unplugged. Did Barbara mention Derek going in to visit her father?"

"No. She just said he'd been there. Things are adding up. I'm going to have a talk with Derek."

"Are you going to tell Sheriff Braxton?"

"I haven't decided yet. But just because he looks as guilty as sin, doesn't mean he is. I wish I knew whether or not he could swim," Robert mused, slowly walking into the parking lot.

Toni followed, her mind perplexed by all that was happening. Was Derek at the bottom of it?

"Sheriff Braxton vaguely mentioned your accident yesterday morning. I guess it still bothers you?"

Toni glanced at him. "I thought I'd gotten over it. But . . ." She took a deep, quivering breath. "I thought it was an accident when the car hit me. Now I'm beginning to wonder. I was visiting Aunt Marge and Uncle Phil a couple of years back. I assumed I'd just picked the wrong time to jog. Now I don't know. I mean, with the car and the dummy I can't help but wonder if it's the same man. I wish I'd seen his face and not just a blur. All I know is that it was a white car."

Toni slowed her walk. "I feel like I'm in the middle of a big mess that I can't comprehend. And I can't stand it when somebody gets away with something like what's happened to Mr. Tankersly—and to me."

Robert's hand enveloped hers. "I'm with you," he said bitterly. His mouth thinned into a grim line, his eyes churning with pain and raw fury. What did his past hold that made anger march across his face like an invading army?

An uneasy silence cloaked them. Toni wished for the light camaraderie they'd experienced at her house two nights ago and yesterday morning at the clinic. Nearing her car, she didn't want to part from him. Toni couldn't explain this feeling, so new to her. But right now going back home to that empty, lonely house held no appeal.

Her car sat only ten feet away. What could she do? *Do something.*

Smiling up at him, she drawled, "So, Cowboy, how long you gonna be in Dodge City?"

He stopped walking and turned to face her. His churning eyes grew glittery with curious laughter, followed by a pair of twitching lips which made the corners of his eyes crease into fine lines. "Just till I sell the rest of them dusty ol' steers, ma'am."

"Long enough for a lady to buy you a steak?" *Where did that come from? I've never asked a man out in my life! What has gotten into me? What if he turns me down? What if he thinks I'm too pushy?*

"I mean, I just thought maybe . . . maybe I could pay . . . pay you back for the pie and all. It was good. I had some for breakfast the last couple of mornings, too, and—"

"You eat pie for breakfast?"

"Well, yes—"

"You know that's not good for you. You should have toast and eggs and—" Robert stopped in midsentence and slowly rubbed his forehead. "I'm starting to sound like my mother."

"You're starting to sound like Uncle Phil. He's always pestering me about my eating habits." Toni shrugged. "I just, well, like different things for breakfast, and lunch, and I guess supper, too."

"And all the snacks in between?"

"Yeah."

Robert laid a hand on her shoulder, his eyes wary and reluctant. "Listen, I'd love to share that steak with you, but I really need to get back to Bobby."

Toni's face warmed like it did during Robert's visit two days ago. She pressed her lips together. Never having blushed in her life, Toni was determined not to start now. She'd just invited a very attractive man to dinner, and he'd just turned her down. Of course, his excuse was legitimate. But Toni sensed Robert would have found another excuse if that one hadn't been available. His eyes were too cautious.

Toni's face cooled. She wouldn't blush. She'd simply go home and melt into a heap of embarrassment. "I understand," she managed to choke out. "I'm sorry. I just thought—"

"Dogies," Robert muttered in consternation. "Why not? I'll call Sylvia and have her pick up Bobby along with Jeff if they get through before I get back."

He tilted his black hat and winked audaciously. "I'd be as happy as a dry field in a rain storm to eat a steak with you, ma'am."

Toni's knees weakened with pleasure. That was the first and last time she'd ask a man out if she had to bite her tongue in half to stop herself. But a tiny, rebellious voice inside her cheered.

CHAPTER 8

Toni chewed the last bite of her steak smothered in spicy sauce. Glancing up she encountered a dark gaze scrutinizing her.

"If you're not full, the menu said they have German chocolate cake. That way you could leave the plate."

Moaning, Toni leaned back. Her stomach felt like a stuffed turkey. "I've had all I can stand."

"You've had all *I* can stand. I don't think I've ever seen a woman eat that much."

Toni narrowed her eyes. "Don't push it! Food and I—we go way back."

The waitress came to clear away the dishes. Toni pulled her billfold from her leather purse and laid enough cash on the ticket to cover the cost.

"I'm gettin' this," Robert said as he went for his billfold.

"No. This was my idea. And I'm paying," she said, smiling.

Robert hesitated, then one side of his mouth lifted. "Okay. But I owe ya one."

"I hoped you'd say that," Toni quipped, wondering if her mouth had suddenly decided to talk without her instigation.

The light mood changed as fast as a bullet leaving a gun's chamber. Robert's gaze snared Toni's in its eternal depth. Her heart jumped in her throat and did cartwheels on the spot. If she ever examined a patient whose heart was doing this, she'd cram a nitroglycerin pill under the poor soul's tongue and call the hospital.

Something magical *had* happened over that cherry cheese pie and coffee. And it was growing.

Robert cleared his throat and glanced at his black hat lying on the table. The low lights shimmered in his dark hair. And Toni wondered if it would spring back into place if she touched it. Curling her fingers in her lap, she forced herself to stare across the restaurant.

A quick movement from Robert drew her attention back to him. He'd just checked his gold watch—again.

Rubbing his mustache he smiled at her apologetically. "I'm thinkin' about Bobby."

"I bet you're a good father."

"I try. I guess that's all anybody can say with a nine year old. That boy's rambunctious."

Thoughts of Bobby made Toni curious about what his mother must have been like. A sharp stab of envy pierced through her. What had Pam possessed to capture a man like Robert? Wanting to banish such thoughts, Toni searched for something to say.

"So . . . how's business?" she asked. "Are there enough domestic disasters in Ouray to keep you busy?"

"I'm stayin' pretty busy. I didn't know how it would go when I moved here last August. But I'm booked till the end of this week with a remodeling job. Last month I did some work in Silverton—"

64

"Oh, so your fame has spread."

He shrugged and smiled. "I wouldn't exactly call it fame, but word's gettin' around. It looks like I'll be tied up till the end of the year anyway."

"Do you leave Bobby with Sylvia while you work?" Toni hadn't failed to notice Robert's acceptance of Sylvia's home as a haven for Bobby. She wondered if Sylvia and Robert were more than friends. After all, Sylvia was an attractive, single mother with a boy about Bobby's age. Robert and she were bound to have lots in common.

Robert smiled. "No. He helps me sometimes. And sometimes I leave him with Mrs. Sellers, my pastor's mother. That's the good thing about this setup. I'm my own boss. And I can take him with me in the summer if I'm not doing anything too complicated. We enjoy our time together. Sometimes he'll find a quiet place and read if he gets bored. He started reading a lot when—" Robert stopped himself in midsentence, his expression back to the wariness she'd seen when she invited him to dinner.

A tiny relief eased Toni's mind. So Robert didn't depend on Sylvia as much as it appeared. But she also sensed that Robert was unusually cautious about something she couldn't quite put her finger on.

A stubborn strand of hair escaped from its metal clip and fell into Toni's eyes. Tucking it behind her ear, Toni decided to ask the question which kept rolling through her thoughts. "Uncle Phil said you used to be a policeman and a paramedic. Why didn't you try to get a job in one of those fields? I don't know if Sheriff Braxton needs anyone, but we could use you at the clinic." Lacing her fingers together, Toni rested her chin on them and looked at him thoughtfully.

Robert blinked in uncertainty and flinched. Glancing across the restaurant, he crinkled and uncrinkled his napkin between forefinger and thumb.

65

Toni felt as if she'd trodden on forbidden land, oblivious of the "No Trespassing" sign until it was too late.

Silence created a massive gulf between them, and Toni watched his eyes nearly hide the pain. Then Robert pressed his lips together in a firm line, inhaled, and darted his gaze back to hers.

"It all has to do with the fact that I've done time in prison," he said in a guarded voice.

Shock splashed over Toni like a bucket of scalding water. She fought not to drop open her mouth in astonishment. His agonized eyes made her school her features into a bland mask.

"Why?"

He looked away. "For nothin'. I was framed." His fists tensed on the table, his eyes narrowing to thin slits. "My police partner—my best friend—was a drug dealer. I didn't know it. I was in the middle of a big drug investigation which got too close for his comfort. So he made . . . arrangements . . ." he paused, adding a nasty twist to his voice, ". . . to make *me* look like the dealer."

Robert licked his lips. "Do you know what it's like to see a cell door closing on you? Closing out your whole life? And everybody believed I was guilty. Everybody. They looked at me like I was trash. And the kids at school started punishing Bobby for my problems. The poor boy had already lost his mother. Now he was losing his father and every friend he had."

Robert scrubbed his hand through his hair. "The only person who believed in me besides my parents was my brother, Michael. He conducted his own investigation, snooping around until he uncovered Wayne."

Taking a deep breath, Robert searched Toni's face. "I don't think I'm ready to go back to a police career. And while I was active on the force, I was on call two weekends of the month for the ambulance service. It's all hooked together in my mind. Either way, I still have bad memories." Hostility radiated from him.

Toni suppressed the urge to wrap her arms around Robert and ease some of his pain. What must it have been like? Stuck in that iron-barred cell, knowing the real criminal ran free. "Is that the reason you came to Ouray? To get away from the bad memories?" she asked gently.

Robert stared across the restaurant, seeming detached from her. "I guess that's part of it." Leaning forward on his elbows, Robert's face softened when he looked at her again. "I guess I oughta be glad it happened because I did turn to God in prison. But I'm confused. There's a part of me that festers like an old sore every time I think about it. I think about the time I was tied up in court and then in prison, and how it affected my parents, and how I wasn't there for Bobby. That time can't be replaced. Do you know I didn't even get to help him with his first bug collection? We'd made big plans to go out like real professionals and find the biggest bugs in Texas."

Gritting his teeth, Robert looked at his plate. "That's why Bobby started readin' so much. I guess he wanted to block out the pain. I've made a vow never to disrupt his life again." His gaze flicked back to hers with a new intensity. "Sometimes I think I hate Wayne Freeman. It isn't good enough that he's in prison. Sometimes, I wish he were dead." Narrowing his eyes, Robert seemed to stare right through her.

Toni blinked at his harsh words and watched him slip into a brooding silence. He slammed the door and shut her out. Did she have the possibility of becoming as bitter as Robert? Toni knew if she yielded to the temptation to fall back into her unforgiving state of mind, those same tormented words could mar her soul. She prayed it wouldn't happen.

Toni hadn't expected Robert to tell her all he had. She

sensed he wasn't the type of man who expressed his feelings at every whim. What had he meant when he said he'd vowed never to disrupt Bobby's life again? Would he consider her a disruption? Tension crept into Toni's heart.

"I'm sorry," she murmured. "I shouldn't have pried."

Robert surfaced from his brooding. "You didn't. You didn't know. . . ." After a few seconds, his stormy eyes cleared to sparkling inkiness. "I think I needed to talk about it anyway."

He leaned back in his chair, the haunted look retreating, leaving an empty shadow in its place. "So what about you? Why are you in Ouray and not at some big hospital somewhere? Your uncle told me you went to Harvard med school. Surely a Harvard grad can find a better position than you've got."

Chuckling, Toni fingered her tea glass. "Uncle Phil doesn't leave anything out, does he?"

"Uh-uh. He also told me you ran track in college. Got a scholarship for it even. Love animals, hate liver, and your favorite dessert is cherry cheese pie—"

"Enough! Enough!" Toni held out her hand in resignation.

A soft, mellow chuckle escaped Robert.

Toni's heart warmed, leaving no room for the worry of her being a disruption for Bobby. So his making her favorite dessert two days ago hadn't been a coincidence.

"So why are you in Ouray and not at a hospital?"

Toni traced a trail of water on her glass with her index finger. "I didn't become a doctor to get rich. I just want to help some people and hopefully have a good influence on one or two of them. At first I thought maybe God wanted me to be a missionary. But I realized that there was a mission field right here in the good ol' USA. Besides, do you know a more beautiful spot in America than Ouray? They don't call it the Switzerland of America for nothing."

"You don't have to tell me that. I came to visit a year ago and decided to stay." Robert paused, his gaze roaming to her hair. "It's not hard to believe you want to help people," he mused. Robert looked back into her eyes. "I can tell you really care. When you were hugging Barbara, I was wishin' you'd been around last July when Bobby cut open his knee."

"When I was hugging Barbara, I was wishing such a sweet-looking woman wasn't married to such a creepy—"

"Hi there, you two," an approaching, male voice said.

Toni looked up to see Derek nearing their table. She glanced cautiously at Robert.

"Follow my lead," he muttered. "What are you doing here?" Robert asked in a friendly voice which hid all traces of his suspicion.

"I came to check on Mr. Tankersly, had a few errands to run, and decided to grab a steak before I head back home."

"We've just been over to check on him, too," Toni said.

"Have a seat." Robert motioned to the chair next to him.

"Can't. I've got one leg out the door. Just wanted to tell you how glad I am that Bobby's signed up for swimming lessons. I know he'll enjoy it."

"Have you signed up?" Robert asked.

Derek's eyes shifted warily, and Toni understood Sheriff Braxton's concern. "No. Swimming's not my bag."

"As much as you fish, man, you oughta make it your bag," Robert said. "What happens if you fall in?"

Derek grinned. "I always wear a life jacket, and I haven't fallen in yet." His smile fading, Derek gazed at Robert. "I sure wish I'd known how to swim two days ago though. It was a good thing you were there."

"I think Mr. Tankersly's going to make it," Toni said. "He's been breathing on his own."

"Has he?" Derek asked. "He was still on his breathing machine when I saw him."

69

"You got in to see him?" Robert asked. "I thought they only let family in."

"Barbara told them I was her son. She knew how much I wanted to see him. Mr. Tankersly and his friends have been coming to my hotel restaurant the whole two years that I've been there." Derek shrugged and looped his thumbs into his jeans pockets. "We're almost like family, anyway."

Toni and Robert shared a quick glance. Was Derek telling the truth?

"Well, gotta go," Derek said, heading toward the door. "See you guys around."

"What do you think?" Toni whispered when Derek was out of hearing range.

Robert shrugged. "Did the nurse tell you who said Derek was Mr. Tankersly's grandson?"

Toni thought a few minutes. "No."

"So Barbara could have told him Derek was her son."

"We need to find out for sure."

"And I still want to know whether or not he can swim. He says he can't, but that just seems unlikely to me. And if he always wears a life jacket, I wonder why he didn't have one on Monday?"

"Good thinking," Toni said, admiring Robert's quick mental capabilities. He must have been an excellent cop. "I wonder who unplugged the ventilator. Was it Derek . . . or someone else?"

"I wonder who's trying to scare you." Robert's eyes glinted in the dim lights.

Inhaling, Toni made an effort to blot out the image of that dummy hanging from the wall. She rubbed her chest. "Do you think it's the same person who ran over me? I mean, with the car and all—it makes me think—"

"I don't know. But you need to be careful, Toni. Have you thought about stayin' with your aunt and uncle?"

Toni narrowed her eyes. "Did Uncle Phil tell you to try to get me to stay with them?"

Robert shrugged. "Not exactly. He just mentioned it."

"Well, I need my space. And Uncle Phil's allergic to birds. I can't just move in on them. Besides, whoever's doing this can get to me there as easily as at home."

Robert tugged on his right ear and smiling, shook his head. "Would it threaten your space if I follow you home and check your house before you lock up for the night?"

"Is this part of your watchdog training?"

"Just consider me your friendly mutt on call, ma'am."

CHAPTER 9

Within minutes, Toni pulled out of the hospital parking lot with Robert's headlights reflecting reassurance in her rearview mirror. If the truth were known, Toni was relieved to know she wouldn't have to face that empty house alone. Once she got in and bolted the doors, she'd feel safe. But Toni didn't relish the idea of going in by herself.

She turned on her cassette tape, hoping the music would calm her fears. The soft saxophone solo enveloped her, soothing her tight nerves.

Wait a minute. I don't own a sax tape.

The saxophone music stopped and a heavy breathing invaded Toni's car through her speaker system. Her heart flip-flopped in her chest like a crazed balloon deflating around a room. The breathing grew louder, the air entering and leaving lungs in reed-like gasps. Toni gripped the steering wheel, her hands sweating against the cool leather.

Pressing her lips together, she reached to push the eject button on her tape deck. Whoever was doing this to her was sick. Just as her finger connected with the metal button, a guttural, demon-like voice filled her ears.

"Interferers die! Interferers die! Interferers die!" The voice grew louder and louder, harsher and harsher, wilder and wilder until it finally said, "And you'll die in my arms."

A scream pressed against Toni's lungs as acid shot into her stomach in burning spurts. With a hand shaking out of control, she slammed her finger against the eject button. The tape jumped from the slot with the click of metal on plastic.

But the voice still rang in Toni's ears. Her lips trembled, and the acid from her stomach shot up her throat.

Lost in fear, Toni concentrated on the yellow stripes in the road. Who was doing this to her, and why?

One hour later, she stood in her kitchen while Robert searched her house. The cassette tape lay on the counter. Toni gnawed her lip and studied the clear, plastic case.

Robert's boots thudded softly as he walked up the hall, came through the living room, and moved toward her. "All's clear."

"Thanks." She looked back at the tape. "Are you going to see the sheriff tomorrow?"

He picked it up. "I'm taking this to him *tonight*." Robert set his lips in a determined line. "If it's any consolation, I think the person responsible for all this only wants to terrorize you. If he's close enough to put a tape in your car, he's close enough to kill you if he wanted to."

Toni wrapped her arms around her midsection, wishing the skin on her back didn't crawl as if someone were watching her from behind. "I appreciate that bit of encouragement," she said with a sarcastic turn of her lips.

He lifted one eyebrow. "Yeah, well, that's what watchdogs are for."

Toni swallowed against the burning in her throat. "Whoever it was knew I went to Durango. I'm glad you went too."

Robert grazed her cheek with the back of his index finger. "Me too," he whispered.

Despite all her fear, a shiver of delight sprouted where his work-roughened finger touched her cheek and spread down her neck and arms, making her toes curl.

"You don't think it was . . ."

"Derek?" Robert asked.

"Yeah."

"I don't know," he mused, "but I'm ready to find some answers. He keeps turning up in too many wrong places at too many wrong times. I—"

Someone pounded on the front door, and Toni jumped.

So did Robert. "Steady there," he mumbled. "Just hang tight." The pounding increased in urgency as Robert approached the door.

"Dad?" a boy's voice yelled. "Dad? Are you in there?"

Toni inhaled and shut her eyes.

"Bobby," Robert said with relief. He opened the door. "What's got you all riled up, Champ? I was just comin' over to—"

"It's Jeff's mom—" Bobby stopped to get a big gulp of air, his cheeks flaming. "She's sick. She's real, real sick."

Forgetting her problems, Toni grabbed her doctor's bag from the front closet and ran across the street with Robert at her side. They arrived to find Sylvia's stocky form lying in the middle of the living room, her long hair sprawled across a black and mauve oriental rug. A teary-cheeked Jeff hovered over her. And a golden cocker spaniel licked her face and whined at Jeff.

"Come here, son," Robert said gently, pulling Jeff aside.

Toni checked Sylvia's pupils. "What happened?" she asked Jeff and Bobby.

74

Jeff took a quivering breath. "Um—she was in here read-ing, and she called me to go get her some—some orange juice."

"We were in Jeff's room playing race cars on his comput-er," Bobby said.

"So I—I waited a few minutes 'cause I was in the middle of finishing the race. And—and I got the orange juice. And when I brought it in here, she was standing up, then she just fell down. And I couldn't get—get her to answer me. Is—is my mom . . ."

"No, sweety," Toni said, patting Jeff's shoulder. "Your mom's going to be fine, I think. But you've got to think hard and tell me if she's ever done this kind of thing before."

"No, well, she's never—never fallen down like this. Sometimes she gets real weak and has to eat, but—"

"That's what I wanted to hear."

Toni looked at Robert as Sylvia turned her head and groaned. "Hypoglycemia. See if you can find the orange juice, and put some sugar in it. We need to get it down her."

Within fifteen minutes, Toni had coaxed the semi-conscious Sylvia to drink enough orange juice to bring her back to full awareness.

"I must have fainted," Sylvia mumbled once she got her bearings.

"Does this happen often?" Toni asked. She motioned for Robert to help her assist Sylvia to the couch. Toni grasped Sylvia's upper arm through her golden sweatshirt, surprised to find a firm rippling of muscle there.

"This is only the second time. It happened once when I was a teenager. Usually it isn't all that bad, and I can con-trol it. But I worked out extra hard tonight. And I've been trying to lose a few pounds, so I didn't eat much dinner."

Robert and Toni settled Sylvia on the couch. "Do you lift weights?" Robert asked.

75

He must have noticed the pronounced biceps too, Toni thought.

"Uh-huh. I started about a year and a half ago."

"Bobby, you and Jeff see if you can rustle up some lunch meat or cheese or something out of the refrigerator," Robert said.

Bobby and Jeff rushed for the kitchen.

"I'll be all right as soon as I get some protein down me." Sylvia rubbed her brow, and Toni noticed Sylvia's hands were larger than most women's. But then so were her feet.

"Good thing we'd made it back," Robert said.

Toni gazed around the living room. Sylvia had decorated it in blues, blacks, and mauves. And the paintings on the wall appeared to be very valuable, right along with the oriental rug, designer drapes, and antique furniture.

After Toni made sure Sylvia had completely recovered, she thoughtfully walked back to her house with Robert and Bobby at her side.

"Would you like a soda, Bobby?" Toni asked as they entered the living room.

"Nah," Bobby mumbled.

"No, ma'am," Robert corrected.

"No, ma'am," Bobby said like a weary parrot. He peered up at his dad from under dark brows. "You're late."

"I know." Robert checked his watch. "Dr. Kirkpatrick and I decided to grab a steak."

Bobby crossed his arms and looked at Toni like a disapproving father-in-law.

"I'll just get that cassette and go, now," Robert said.

Toni shook her head, and retrieved the tape from the bar, the room so full of tension she thought it would explode. Bobby wasn't happy about her and Robert's new friendship. And Toni couldn't say she blamed him. After all, Bobby had already lost his father once. Any threat on his time with Robert probably scared him.

"What's up doc?" Tweety Bird asked from his cage. *What's up? Someone just threatened my life—again. And the only man I've ever been strongly attracted to has a little boy who can't stand the sight of me.*

"Cool!" Bobby said, his face losing some of its disapproving lines as he watched Tweety Bird. He walked over to the cage and peaked in on the bird.

"Yeah," Robert said, following him. "He says all sorts of things."

"Like what?" Bobby asked.

Toni moved toward the cage. "Like, 'Go, Red Skins, go.' "

Tweety Bird let out a long wolf whistle and repeated Toni.

"We don't like the Red Skins," Bobby said. "We like the Dallas Cowboys."

"Oh well, champ," Robert said, roughing up Bobby's hair. "Somebody's got to be for the losing team." He winked at Toni.

"The losing team? I'll have you know—"

"I'm ready to go home," Bobby said, interrupting what was about to turn into a playful teasing session.

Robert cleared his throat and took the cassette from Toni. "We're going, Bobby."

"Wait," Toni said, wanting to mention a couple of odd things to Robert. "I . . . um . . . there's something I need to tell you before you go." She glanced at Bobby. "Something about . . . what we were talking of over dinner."

Bobby was not going to be happy about this, but Toni couldn't discuss murder in front of a nine year old. Maybe her observations were clues. Maybe not. But this might be the last time Toni saw Robert for a while, and she'd never call him. Not after asking him out. He'd think she was pushing herself on him.

"Bobby, why don't you go out on the porch for a few seconds?"

"D-a-d!"

Robert gently pushed Bobby toward the door. "I'll only be a minute."

"Why can't I stay?"

"We've got to talk about some grownup stuff. Now don't cause a scene, son."

Bobby opened the door. "I don't know why you want to talk to some ol' girl anyway. Girls are sissies."

"Excuse me for a minute," Robert said, following Bobby outside.

The soft rumble of Robert's voice drifted into Toni. She couldn't tell what he said, but she could just imagine. Boy, had she started on the wrong foot with Bobby or what. Not only was his father spending time with her, but Bobby was getting into trouble over her. *Way to go, Kirkpatrick.*

"Robert's a hunk," Tweety Bird chimed.

"Oh be quiet," Toni snapped.

"Be quiet," Tweety Bird repeated.

Toni blinked. That was a new one for her feathered friend. She must have been telling him to be quiet more than she'd thought. The longer she had him the more he said and the faster he seemed to be picking up new phrases.

Robert walked back into the living room and closed the door. "Sorry."

"I hope you weren't too hard on him. I know he didn't mean it."

"Oh, he meant it, all right. And you're going to get an apology."

Toni placed her hand on Robert's arm. "No, don't make him apologize—"

"He's going to apologize." Robert raised his brows, a determined glint in his eyes' black depths. "There's no excuse for his being so rude."

Toni swallowed, a sinking feeling in her stomach. "I made a vow never to disrupt Bobby's life again," Robert had said over dinner. Toni had questioned then if she'd be a disruption. Tonight gave her a qualified yes.

"I just wondered what you thought about Sylvia being so muscular and having rather large hands. You said the only way a woman could have made such deep marks on Mr. Tankersly's neck was if—"

"She lifted weights." Robert's eyes glowed with a new respect. "Good point. But what would be her motive? Does she even know Mr. Tankersly?"

"Maybe you could find out. And one other thing. She doesn't work, does she?"

"Not that I know of."

"Where did she get the money to furnish her house like that?"

"I wondered that the first time I was over there. Initially I thought maybe her ex-husband paid exceptionally good child support. Then I found out she was widowed. Maybe her husband had a healthy life insurance policy. Or she might have come from a wealthy family—old money, or somethin'."

"You're probably right." Toni inhaled and crossed her arms. "I think I'm getting paranoid. I mean, why would Sylvia Cornelius want to kill Mr. Tankersly?"

Robert shrugged. "Who knows? Your observations probably won't amount to anything, but I'm going to check into them anyway. Whoever did it has to fit 'murder number one,' whatever that means."

He paused as if he were trying to decide whether or not to speak his thoughts. "You have my business card. Call me if anything else happens, you hear?"

Toni shook her head. *So in other words, you won't be calling me.* Well, he didn't have to worry about her calling him, either. She'd survived thirty years without Robert Hooper in her life. Why did she need him now?

"Promise?"

Swallowing, Toni looked into his eyes as silence stretched between them.

"That's what I thought," he mumbled, a derisive smile cocking one side of his mouth. "Would it help you to know your watchdog thinks you're beautiful?"

Toni tried to pull her suddenly dry tongue away from the roof of her mouth. "Thanks," she whispered, her heart pounding in her ears. Why did she need him now? About a hundred reasons flashed through her mind.

And if Toni didn't know any better, she'd think the man wanted to kiss her. His gaze trailed to her lips and stayed there far too long for Toni's peace of mind.

Instead he said, "Let me get Bobby. You've got an apology coming."

CHAPTER 10

The next morning, Robert milled around in the hardware store, trying to remember why he'd come in there. The smell of garden hoses and fertilizer didn't do anything to keep his mind from shifting into a gear other than the one he needed it in—a gear labeled Toni Kirkpatrick.

What was he going to do? Robert didn't want to make Bobby miserable. But at the same time, he'd grown dissatisfied with his life ever since Toni's smile had knocked him off his feet. Robert missed having a woman in his life more than he'd realized. He knew he'd never forget Pam. Robert had loved her dearly, but he needed someone to hold again, someone who was his. Now, *he* was miserable.

And the fact that someone was threatening Toni only added to his misery. Would she be murdered before he'd barely gotten to know her? Robert had to do everything in his power to figure out what was going on. That included a trip to Derek's hotel and a call to Barbara Jones today.

A tired voice cut into his thoughts. "What do you need this morning, Robert?"

Turning toward the voice, Robert saw Doug Tankersly, dressed in a blue cardigan, walking down the cluttered store aisle toward him. Doug's eyes were sunken in their tired sockets, and dark fatigue lines marked his face—making him look decisively older than he had last night.

Robert smiled. "How's your father?"

"He made it through the night. It was touch and go after you and the doctor left. But he stabilized this morning about four. His doctor thinks he might make it after all," he stated flatly.

"That's great," Robert said. "Looks like all our prayers paid off."

Doug shrugged. "Probably luck. Daddy always was the lucky one." Doug glanced past Robert to a woman who was looking at varnish.

Robert frowned. Doug acted as if he didn't care one way or the other about his father's life. Robert cleared his throat. "I—came in for a couple of new paint brushes."

Doug helped Robert find the brushes he wanted and checked him out. By the time Robert paid for his merchandise, he decided Doug was in the same sphere with Frank—*Twilight Zone* material, both of them. Robert slipped his change into his jeans pocket and turned to leave.

"Robert?"

He turned to face Doug.

A hesitant, weary smile played on Doug's face. "Thanks for saving Dad. I don't think I've told you, but I appreciate what you and Derek did."

Robert smiled in relief. Maybe Doug wasn't as strange as Frank after all. Perhaps he was simply exhausted. "I'm just glad I was there. Otherwise . . ." He shrugged. "Anybody else would've done the same thing."

Robert started to turn and leave, but hesitated. Should he ask Doug about Derek's visit to Mr. Tankersly? It couldn't hurt. "Derek mentioned he got in to see your dad last night. Do you remember his asking?"

Doug blinked in surprise. "No. They were only supposed to let family in to see him. Visiting hours are so short. . . . But then I wasn't there as long as Barbara was. I'd only been there about an hour when you and the doctor showed up. Maybe you better ask Barbara. But I can't imagine them letting Derek back there.

"I wish I knew who was behind this. It's got us all worried stiff. Did you know somebody unplugged his breathing machine?" Doug asked.

"That's what Toni said. I was really sorry to hear that."

Doug shook his head and stared out the window.

"Could I ask just one more thing? Then I'll be gone."

"Sure."

"Do you know if your father knew Sylvia Cornelius?"

"Sylvia Cornelius?" Doug squinted his eyes and looked up as if he were trying to remember her himself.

" 'Bout this tall, long brownish-blond hair, blue eyes, stocky, pretty—"

"Oh! Yes he did as a matter of fact. She used to work as a waitress at Derek's restaurant when he first moved here two years back. Dad and his buddies started meeting there for dominoes almost as soon as Derek opened the hotel."

"Excuse me," Gordon Jones said from behind Robert.

Robert turned to face him.

"Did you say someone unplugged Mr. Tankersly's breathing machine?"

Robert nodded and started to speak, but Doug beat him to it. "You mean Frank didn't tell you?"

"No." Gordon swallowed, the color draining from his face. "How could someone do that?" he asked in his soft

83

voice. "I mean, I just can't imagine. I—" He stopped as if he were trying to regain composure of his trembling voice.

"The RN told Toni he thought maybe it was the maid," Robert said.

"Is that what you think?" Gordon asked.

Robert shrugged. "I don't know what to think."

Gordon rubbed the back of his neck where his brown hair barely touched his tan shirt's collar. "Man! This is getting spooky. It's like a late night movie or something."

Doug took a deep, weary breath. "Yeah. And I hope it's cut short."

"Same here," Robert said.

"Mr. Tankersly has almost been like the father I never had," Gordon said, his voice still unsteady. "I—I just don't know how I'll take it if he doesn't come out of this."

Robert placed a hand on Gordon's shoulder. "Let's hope he does."

Doug glanced at the customers milling around the store.

"Well, I guess I need to get on with my job," Robert said.

"I'm waiting on Frank to get here, Doug," Gordon said. "He's helping me with my plumbing. My house flooded last night. You go ahead and wait on your customers."

Doug walked toward an old man standing beside a shovel display. "Thanks again," he said as Robert walked toward the door.

Robert nodded and maneuvered his way through the narrow aisles and out onto the sidewalk. So Sylvia knew Mr. Tankersly. And she knew Derek, too. Of course, that wasn't a crime, but it definitely made her a possible suspect, especially since she was into weight lifting. But did she have a motive?

Robert toyed with this thought as he walked toward his red truck.

"You," a hate-filled voice said from a few feet down the sidewalk.

84

Robert jerked up his head to spot the source of the voice. A pair of flinty eyes stared back.

"Yeah. I'm talking to you," Frank Jones spat, nearing Robert.

Robert stopped, the muscles in his arms and legs tightening as if he were going to battle. Maybe he was. He'd never seen so much hate in a man's face. "What exactly did you want to talk about?" Robert asked softly.

Frank positioned himself only inches from Robert and glared up into his face. "If you'd just minded your own business, we wouldn't be in this mess," Frank accused, his face contorting in anger. "If anybody deserved to die, it was Jacob Tankersly."

Robert's heart lurched, beating against his ribs like a machine gun. *Was Frank the one?*

"But no. You came along and did your good deed for the day." Pushing past Robert, Frank walked toward the store. "Keep your nose in your own business next time, cowboy," he called over his shoulder as he jerked on the hem of his blue sweater vest.

Robert's muscles tensed even tighter. He'd get Frank and haul him into the sheriff for questioning if he had to tackle him. "Hey! Come back here!"

Ignoring Robert, Frank walked into the hardware store, slamming the door behind him. The welcome bell rang angrily.

Robert lunged for the door, whipping it open. The noisy bell caused several early morning shoppers to turn and look at him in curiosity. Robert stood on the threshold, staring at Frank's retreating back. Starting to yell at him again, Robert stopped with his mouth open. Every person in the store stared at him. He slowly remembered he wasn't the one responsible for hauling in Frank. Reluctantly, Robert backed out of the doorway, closing the door behind him.

Wheeling around, he ran for his truck. Frank could be

the answer to who tried to kill Mr. Tankersly. Had he been terrifying Toni, too?

Within minutes, Robert burst through the sheriff's office door, banging it against the wall. The office smelled of stale coffee and musty papers. Scanning the room, his gaze settled on a red-haired young woman sitting behind a messy desk.

"Sheriff Braxton in?" he demanded. Striding to the desk, he towered over her.

"No. He stepped out for a moment," the young woman said.

"When do you expect him back? Where'd he go? Maybe I can catch up with him."

The secretary blinked. "Maybe you'd like to wait on him. He or one of the deputies should be back any minute."

What if Frank was the one? If given enough time, he could ride off into the sunset without ever answering a question. Robert slammed his hand against the desk top. "No! I don't have time to wait!"

The secretary jumped and stared up at him.

Exhaling, Robert took off his hat and scraped his hand through his hair. *You've done it again, ol' boy. Jumped in with both feet like a pig-headed—* "I'm sorry," he said gently. "But it's important."

"Robert!" Sheriff Braxton boomed from the doorway.

Robert swiveled toward the red-cheeked sheriff, relaxing somewhat at the sight of his stout frame.

"Just the man I wanted to see," the sheriff said, nearing Robert. Extending his hand, he grabbed Robert's and pumped it. "I'm in need of a deputy and Dr. Weston says you might help me. He says you have a degree in criminal justice and experience to boot."

Robert gripped his hat in urgency. *Don't the people in this town ever stop with the job offers?* Sweeping aside his suggestion, Robert glanced at the secretary then back to the sheriff. "I need to talk to you somewhere in private."

Sheriff Braxton clapped Robert's shoulder. "Step right into my office, son, and we'll talk. I knew there was somethin' special about you when you moved here almost a year ago. But then today the doc tells me you were a policeman in Texas, and I knew you were my man."

He turned at the office door to look at his secretary. "Alice, this is the man who saved ol' Jake Tankersly from drowning."

"Really?" Alice said, not sounding nearly as impressed as Sheriff Braxton. She opened her mouth as if she wanted to say more, but decided against it. Robert assumed he hadn't made the best impression on her.

Forgetting Alice, he gripped the sheriff's arm, urged him into the office, and snapped the door shut.

"Whoa there, son," Sheriff Braxton croaked. "What's got you in such an uproar?"

"I've got a lead on who tried to kill Mr. Tankersly," Robert snapped.

The sheriff's tawny eyes bugged as he grabbed Robert's arm. "Who?"

"Frank Jones, his son-in-law. He just as much told me he hated Jacob, and—"

"He didn't do it," Sheriff Braxton said, slumping into his chunky office chair and shaking his head.

"How do you know he didn't do it?" Robert's ears almost roared with frustration. "Listen to me. I met him on the street about five minutes ago, and he told me I should've let Jake drown. Said he *deserved* to die. I don't know about you, but I think that's a pretty good reason to at least question him." For the first time since he'd quit the force, Robert wanted to take over a case and solve it.

"Sit down there, boy." The sheriff pointed to a straight-backed chair across from him and propped his feet on the corner of his disorganized desk. "I already have questioned him. Questioned him the day 'fore yesterday, as a matter of fact. And he's got an alibi that's airtight. He'd have to be able to split in two if he was the murderer."

Robert crammed one hand into his jeans pocket and dropped his hat on the chair. Grinding his teeth together, he studied his teak-colored boots, dissatisfaction settling over him.

Maybe Robert was right in suspecting Derek or Sylvia. Maybe Frank wasn't even involved. Maybe he just disliked his father-in-law for some reason. In-law dissent isn't uncommon.

"Where was he?" Robert asked.

"At Harry's Diner. Sitting at his usual table, having his usual lunch like he does every day. A whole restaurant full of people saw him, including Harry himself." Sheriff Braxton crossed his arms.

Robert rubbed his eyes. "Have you thought about the possibility of Frank's hiring someone to kill Jake?"

"Yep. No evidence. And besides, Frank doesn't have the kind of money it'd take to hire a hit man. Neither does anybody else in that family for that matter."

"Sorry. I didn't mean to come in here and tell you how to do your job." He glanced around the office, noticing how its rough-hewn walls reflected the sheriff's rugged personality.

"That's fine, son. I like that in a policeman. To tell you the truth, Frank was the first person I thought of myself. I mean, everybody knows there's no love lost between ol' Jake and Frank."

Standing, Sheriff Braxton walked across the room and peered out the only window in the office. "Even though Frank and Barbara have been married twenty-five years, Frank and Jake still can't stand each other. See, ol' Jake has a lot of money locked safely away, and he won't let either of his children touch it. He lives with Barbara and Frank, and he won't even give Barbara any help for his upkeep. So I know Frank's got a good motive, but I don't have any evidence." He faced Robert.

"Is there a will?"

"Yeah. There's a will all right. But Doug's the one who benefits the most. It all goes back to Jake not liking Frank. Don't get me wrong, Barbara will still come out with a fat chunk. It's just that Doug comes out better."

Robert rubbed his right ear thoughtfully. "Wonder why Barbara takes care of her father like that when there's so much tension? Why doesn't she just let Doug take him?"

The sheriff scratched his head and messed up his already spiky hair. "Marge says Barbara promised her mother she'd take care of him. Her mother died a couple of years ago, and Barbara's kept her promise."

Robert frowned. Looked like the sheriff's laid-back attitude hid a sharp law officer. Robert reminded himself again he wasn't the one in charge of this case, and it really wasn't any of his business. However, Toni Kirkpatrick and her safety were his business. And the sooner this case was solved, the sooner her safety returned.

Robert knew the time had come to tell Sheriff Braxton about Derek and Sylvia. Too much added up, and the sheriff needed all the pieces before he could put this puzzle together.

Robert picked up his hat from the chair, placed it on the desk, and sat down. "You said you had a motive and no evidence with Frank. Well, I've got some circumstantial evidence but no motive on a couple of people," Robert said, rubbing his hand down his jeans-clad thigh.

"I wondered when you were going to get around to telling me what you knew." Braxton resumed his seat.

Robert jerked his gaze to the sheriff. "How'd you—"

"I done told you once, son. I ain't been in this business forty years without knowing how to read people."

89

Robert shook his head, chuckled, then told the sheriff all his observations. " . . . the only thing I still don't know is whether or not Derek can swim and why Sylvia went to work as a waitress when she apparently didn't need the money."

"Maybe she needed a man."

"What?"

"Rumor had it Sylvia and Derek had something going right after he moved into these parts."

"Oh really? Now that's interesting." Robert propped his right ankle on his left knee. Sylvia might be a bigger part of this picture than he'd originally thought. "You said 'had something going.' I guess that means they're history."

"Yeah. And the grapevine says he's the one who broke it off. They say he broke her heart."

"So maybe he isn't as nice a guy as everybody thinks."

"Maybe not."

Robert stood and picked up his hat. "I'm goin' to try to call Barbara today and check out Derek's story about her telling the nurse he was Jake's grandson. And I'll see if I can find out whether or not Derek can swim. I'll do a little snoopin' around Derek's place and see what I come up with." He stopped for a second. "That is, if you don't mind."

"Nah. I don't mind. It'll look less conspicuous if you do it anyway. Just let me know what you uncover, you hear? I'm going to see if I can find out where Sylvia was at the time of Jake's drowning."

"Sounds good." Robert picked up the toy car lying on the desk. "Whoever did it has to connect with 'murder number one.' "

"Whatever that means."

"What do you make of the cassette tape?" Robert asked, staring at the red paint on the toy car's hood.

"I think Dr. Kirkpatrick needs to be careful. Sounds like

the man is *really* interested in her . . . if you know what I mean"

"I know. I don't like any of this, but his saying she'll die in his arms sounds . . . pretty sick." Robert hadn't said anything to Toni, but he was starting to wonder if this creep had some fixation for her. "Do you think it's the same person who ran over her, or the person who tried to kill Mr. Tankersly? He could remember Toni's accident and just be trying to scare her."

Braxton rubbed his hand across his mouth. "I wish I knew. I wish I'd been able to figure out who ran over her. That's bothered me for two years. But short of standing everyone who's lived here the last two years in a line and—"

"Wait a minute. Derek's only been here two years."

"I know."

"What color car does he drive?"

"A red convertible Mercedes."

"A convertible Mercedes. Those things cost about a hundred grand!"

"That's right."

"I know the hotel business can be profitable, but he only owns one small hotel, not a whole chain."

Sheriff Braxton nodded.

"Was he driving it when he moved here?"

"Nope. Up until about nine months ago, he had a red Ford. Must have a thing for red or something," the sheriff said without blinking an eye.

"I wonder where he got that kind of money?"

"Tell me where Sylvia got hers."

Robert and the sheriff shared a long, contemplative glance.

Shrugging, Sheriff Braxton stood. "There's a lot I still don't know about this case, but I do know it's a good thing you're keeping an eye on the doc."

91

Robert placed the toy car back on the old oak desk. "Yeah. I need to get back to work."

Braxton strode toward Robert and slapped his back. "I'm mighty glad you came."

Robert nodded. "I guess Doug, Barbara, and Gordon have alibis, too," he said on a hunch. Robert didn't much think Gordon fit into this picture. He was an in-law at all angles except with Frank, but you never knew.

Smiling, the sheriff pointed at him. "I knew I liked you. Yep. Three of Doug's customers and his one employee say Doug was in his hardware store not too long before you brought ol' Jake in. Barbara was at home by herself, but she and Frank only have the one car. And Frank had it. Gordon had some business to take care of in Montrose. Barbara and Frank confirmed his story." He shrugged. "That takes care of everybody."

Robert smiled in self-derision. "Sorry. I had to ask."

" 'Course you did. Doesn't surprise me one bit. It comes natural to you, I imagine. That's why I say you're my man. I need a deputy. And word's spread 'round about how you saved Jake. You might not know it, but you're a hero in this town. And if we can get you in here and get the people familiar with seeing you around, when I retire in the fall, you can run for sheriff. That no-good Buster Sniper thinks he's gonna sweep the election with me retirin'. But he can't win against the likes of you. Yep—"

"Sorry, Sheriff, but I'm not interested. I've started this handyman business, and it's goin' too well to stop."

"Not interested! 'Course you're interested. I can see interest oozin' out all over you." He looked up at Robert in disbelief. "What's the matter with you? You were born to be in law enforcement, looks to me like, not to be a handyman."

Robert suppressed a grin. How much more direct could a person be? Sheriff Braxton would be a real hoot to work for.

A murky shadow blotted out the smile. No. He wouldn't even think about going back into law enforcement. After a week or two of all those memories swamping him, Robert would be like a furious bull pawing the ground. He couldn't take it. Too much pain.

"The answer's still no." Robert smiled in an attempt to soften the blunt words. "I'm sure you'll find somebody. It just isn't me."

Sheriff Braxton shook his head. "I won't push it for now. But be warned—"

"See you 'round." Robert crammed his hat on and headed for the door.

"I won't take no for an answer," Sheriff Braxton called.

CHAPTER 11

Two days later. "Hello." Toni dropped her keys, purse, and bag of new clothes on the couch. She'd been out for a Saturday afternoon shopping spree and came home to a ringing telephone.

"Hey Toni. Thought you might want an update."

Toni swallowed. She hadn't heard from Robert since Wednesday. That had been three days, and she was beginning to think he'd come to the same, safe conclusion she had—they had zero potential for a good relationship.

"Sure. What did you find out?" Toni removed her teal sweater vest from its matching plaid shirt. The afternoons were starting to get warmer.

"Well, still no news on Derek's swimming. But I've been trying to get in touch with Barbara since Thursday morning. I finally talked with her last night."

"And?"

"And, she said she didn't tell the RN that Derek was her son. Said she didn't even know Derek had gone in to see her father."

"Things are starting to add up."

"Yeah. And boy was Barbara mad when she found out Derek had been into the ICU without her knowing it."

"Does Derek know she denied his claim?"

"Yeah. But he's stuck to what he said in the first place. Sheriff Braxton's supposed to be calling the RN you talked with to verify Barbara's story."

Toni licked her lips. "Does she have any motive for Derek to kill her father?"

"No. All she said was what we already knew. Mr. Tankersly and his buddies met at the hotel for dominoes."

"Do you think Derek's involved in something Mr. Tankersly found out about?"

"That's what I've been asking myself. But what? And how does 'murder number one' fit in?"

"That's the key," Toni said, watching Sylvester paw at something behind the overstuffed, beige chair sitting against the wall. He stuck his nose toward the floor then jerked it back.

"If we could just figure that out. . . ." Robert trailed off thoughtfully. "And another thing I thought you might find interestin'—Derek and Sylvia used to be involved. When he first moved here, she worked for him."

Toni picked up the peach-colored telephone and walked toward the chair, intent on discovering what Sylvester clawed for.

". . . also, Frank and Jacob seem to have a rivalry going. They can't stand each other. Braxton says Frank has a good motive, but he also has a good alibi."

Toni listened to Robert as she scooted the chair away from the wall and peered behind it. Sylvester hissed as something dark lunged forward, aiming for the cat, but hit-

95

ting Toni's jeans clad leg with a blunted bump.

Toni's stomach churned with terror, her heart slamming against her breast. She screamed, dropped the phone, and jumped back as a serpent slithered sideways, preparing itself for another strike.

Toni stumbled into her end table and fell between the couch and wicker coffee table. The snake reared back, opened his mouth wide, and threw itself at the bottom of her right shoe. Toni felt the blow like death itself.

Another scream tore from her as Sylvester batted the serpent's tale. It turned on the cat, striking again and again. But Sylvester dodged the snake each time.

Toni's throat burned with acid as she scrambled from the floor and climbed onto the couch with legs wobbling like over-cooked pasta. Unable to stop the horror, another scream ripped from her. Shaking out of control, Toni gulped for air, her skin crawling.

As the snake beat a retreat toward the chair, she noticed the diamond-shaped designs on its back for the first time. Sylvester, hot on his trail, wouldn't give the serpent one moment's rest.

It's a rattlesnake! But why hadn't it rattled? And why didn't it bite her? The thing tried for all it was worth.

She stared at the chair for a full five minutes, knowing she was going to have to get the hoe out of the storage shed and kill the snake before it got away and hid elsewhere in the house. Having only killed two snakes in her life, Toni wasn't an expert snake killer. But the job had to be done.

The front door banged open against the wall. And jumping, Toni screamed again.

"What happened?" Robert asked, rushing toward her, his eyes gleaming black with fear. Bobby entered more reluctantly, a baseball glove on his right hand.

"Don't come in here!" Toni yelled, holding her hand out

to him, and running to the other end of the couch. "There's a snake—I think it's a rattlesnake."

Sylvester hissed and stuck his paw under the chair, trying to fish the serpent back out.

Without a word, Robert grabbed Toni, lifted her over the couch's back, and deposited her next to him. "Get outside," he ordered. "You too, Bobby." He pushed Toni toward the door. "Do you have a hatchet or axe around here?"

"No. I've got a hoe in the storage building." Toni motioned to a portable building sitting to the side of her house.

"Good enough." Robert rushed toward the structure.

Toni stood on the porch with Bobby while Robert entered the house. She heard Robert's boots scuff against the hardwood floor as he cornered the snake. Then a chopping noise followed. Toni never thought the sound of a hoe against her newly varnished floors would ever be so welcome.

Bobby peered through the living room window. "He killed it."

"Toni? Go get the shovel," Robert said.

"Don't know why you couldn't've gotten somebody else to kill it," Bobby mumbled just loud enough for Toni to hear. "It was just a stupid ol' snake."

Just a stupid ol' snake! Toni bit her tongue, trying to stop the short retort ready to leap out, and went to get the shovel for Robert.

"It's a rattlesnake, all right," Robert said a few moments later when he stood on the porch, holding the shovel with the snake in it.

"But it doesn't have any rattlers," Toni said.

"They've been removed. Right along with his fangs."

"What?"

"His mouth opened while I was—"

"Murdering him?"

Robert smiled. "Yeah. I thought maybe I just couldn't see

97

the fangs what with the sun setting and only the lamp on. But after I finished him off, I used a pencil to make sure. No fangs."

The hairs on Toni's arm rose at the sight of the long reptile lying lifeless in the shovel. "That's why he couldn't bite me."

"He got close enough to bite you?"

"Why do you think I was screaming?" Toni shivered and pressed her lips together.

Propping the shovel beside the steps, Robert allowed the dead serpent to rest on the ground beside it. "Looks like you could use a hug." He wrapped his arms around her.

Toni willingly went into their warm safety, her heart's pace increasing as the rough texture of Robert's fuchsia, broadcloth shirt rubbed against her cheek.

Bobby slipped back into the house, the screen door closing behind him.

"It's bad enough that someone's trying to scare me without wildlife getting in on the deal."

"I think wildlife had some help this time."

Toni pulled away from his rapid heartbeat and sandal-wood smell. "What?"

His hand engulfed hers. "Come back in here."

Toni walked into the living room behind Robert. Bobby stood with his back to them and studied Tweety Bird. Toni knew Bobby had seen Robert hug her, and he probably wasn't happy about it. But at the moment she hadn't thought about their audience, and Toni supposed Robert hadn't either. Things like snakes in your living room had a tendency to slow down your thought process.

Loosening his grip on her hand, Robert walked across the room. "See this window?" He pointed to the one next to her rock fireplace.

"It's got a hole in it." Noticing the few shards of glass

lying on the floor, Toni swallowed.

"Uh-huh. Just big enough for a snake to be dropped through. And look at this." Robert picked up a small, toy car from under the window and held it up for Toni's inspection.

Her stomach churned. It was identical to the one she'd found on her porch. "He wanted me to know who was behind this, too."

"That's right. And whoever did it made sure the snake didn't have any rattlers, so you wouldn't be warned, and any fangs, so he couldn't really hurt you."

"Just scare me to death?"

"Right."

"I treated a patient one time who had a massive heart attack over a snake."

"The way you sounded, I thought you were going to."

"How'd you get here so fast?"

"I live just two streets over."

"Small world."

"Small town," Robert said, smiling.

Bobby, who'd been listening intently, turned wide eyes to Robert. "Somebody *put* the snake in here?"

"Right," Robert said cautiously.

"And that car?"

"Right."

"Why?"

Toni and Robert shared a lengthy glance. "It's a long story, Champ."

"Somebody doesn't like Dr. Kirkpatrick? Why not?"

Toni wasn't sure whether or not Bobby sounded truly curious or just plain glad.

"We don't know," Robert said. "But we've got to get you over to the Martins' or you're going to be late for Sam's birthday party."

Bobby peered up at Toni.

99

"See you around," Toni said, giving Bobby her brightest smile.

Bobby didn't return the smile. "Right," he said, walking out the doorway, letting the screen door shut behind him.

"Stay tuned. We're pausing for station identification. We'll be right back," Robert said, heading for the door.

"You're coming back?"

"You don't think I'm gonna leave you here by yourself, do you? Somebody's got to board up that window and—act as watchdog. Besides, we need to call the sheriff about this. He might be able to get some prints."

"I'll call him while you're gone," Toni said, picking up the phone from where she'd dropped it.

"And you might let your aunt and uncle know what's goin' on, too."

"No," Toni said, shaking her head. "They'll worry. Then they'll tell Mom and Dad. And Dad will try to get me to move back to Arkansas."

"That might not be a bad idea, except—"

"No," Toni said emphatically. She'd never run from anything in her life. And she wasn't going to start now. What if someone decided he or she didn't like her in Arkansas? Where would she run to then?

"Okay," Robert said, raising his brows. "I give." He pushed open the door to leave, turned to look at Toni again, and cleared his throat. "The real reason I called was . . . I've got stuff to make hamburgers with. And it's gonna be a mighty long evenin', what with the boy gone off to this birthday party." He smiled slowly. "Care to join me?"

Toni hesitated. Common sense told her not to become too friendly with Robert because she might wind up getting hurt. It was obvious Bobby didn't approve of the friendship between her and Robert, and just as obvious that Robert wouldn't do anything to upset his son. This was a dead-end situation. Where could it lead?

"Sure," Toni heard herself say. It could lead to an evening she wouldn't forget.

CHAPTER 12

A few hours later, Toni sank to the sprawling hearth surrounding Robert's rugged, rock fireplace. Picking up the long, metal poker propped to the side, she jabbed at the glowing coals and inhaled the smell of oak on fire.

Robert was getting more wood, and Toni's muscles were finally relaxing after a warm meal and light conversation with Robert. She glanced around the living room which smacked of male habitation and wished she could throw a peach pillow in the corner of the blue tweed sofa and hang a few paintings. Even though it lacked frills, the whole house was neat—something Toni couldn't boast of.

Robert stomped through the kitchen door, arms full of wood. Dodging the furniture, he dropped his burden into the large, cedar wood box beside Toni, then brushed the wood particles off his fuchsia broadcloth shirt and black jeans.

"This is nice," Toni said. "I haven't built a fire yet because I don't have any wood. I think I'll see about getting some tomorrow. When it's cool like tonight, a fire's nice."

"I'll give you some of mine," Robert said, throwing two logs on the fire.

"That's all right. I can—"

"Now listen. I've got enough wood out back for all of Dallas. I won't miss a stick or two for you." His teeth gleamed in a coaxing smile as he sat on the floor and leaned against the hearth. "Besides, any lady who smells as good as you do should get anything she wants."

Good grief. When the man smiled like that, Toni would agree to being burned at the stake. "It won't run you short?" she asked, secretly delighted he'd noticed her new citrusy perfume.

"Nah," he said, turning to stab the blazing logs with the long poker. Swiveling back to face her, Robert rubbed his mustache.

"Pretty jewelry," he said, pointing to her earrings.

"Thanks." Toni's ears ached from the clips, and she pulled them off. Massaging her ear lobes with one hand, Toni examined the earrings lying in her palm. The firelight exploded in their emerald depths.

"When Grandma Weston died, she left me all her jewelry." Toni's heart moved with memories. "I used to admire it when I was a little girl, and she'd always say, 'It'll all be yours someday.' "

Toni glanced up at Robert. "Now it is. And I think of her every time I put on a piece. It's almost like she's with me."

Robert nodded. "My father gave me a lifetime's tools. And even though he's still alive, I feel the same way when I use one of them. It's a nice feeling."

They sat in companionable silence for a few minutes, neither one talking. Toni relished knowing she didn't have to make conversation with Robert to enjoy his company.

"Did you call to find out about Mr. Tankersly today?" Robert asked, breaking the quietness.

"Yeah. I did. At about two-thirty they said he was still unconscious. But he's some better." Thoughts of Mr. Tankersly conjured up her own problems, and a new desperation engulfed her. Would she survive until they found out who was behind this? Would she be able to hold off the flood of bitterness that threatened to take its former place in her heart?

Toni swallowed as the temptation to strangle the person who put that snake in her house almost overwhelmed her. No. She couldn't let herself slip back into the old pattern. Her physical life might be under threat, but so was her spiritual well-being. And she'd fight for both.

"I hope he pulls through," Robert said.

"Do you think the sheriff can make anything out of that blue piece of fuzz he found on my window screen?" Toni asked, referring to the one and only clue Sheriff Braxton and Robert had discovered around her broken window.

Robert shrugged. "It's not much, but it's all we've got, especially since there weren't any fingerprints."

Toni grimaced, thinking about the mess Sheriff Braxton made. "I don't know if I'll ever get all that black powder off my drapes." The fine powder he'd used clung to everything it came in contact with.

"I've got an idea," Robert said. He stood and walked toward the cherry rolltop desk sitting by the front window. "When I was on the force and needed to solve a case, I used to write out all the clues and observations I had. Sometimes seeing it on paper would make something click." He sat down beside her, legal pad and pen in hand. "The criminal may have already hanged himself, and all we need to do is see it."

"Good idea." Toni clipped the earrings back on her lobes, then pushed up the sleeves of her dark green sweater.

"Okay. Our first clue is 'Murder Number One.' " He wrote it down.

"Derek was at the sight. He says he can't swim," Toni said. "He says he always wears a life jacket, but he didn't have one on."

"Derek has only been here two years."

"My accident took place two years ago."

"But he doesn't drive a white car. Drives a red Mercedes convertible. Until nine months ago drove a red Ford."

"A Mercedes convertible?" Toni asked, her mouth open. "Those things cost about—about—"

"A hundred grand."

"Where'd he get that kind of money?"

"My reaction exactly. Sheriff Braxton says he doesn't know."

"I know the hotel business can be profitable. But I wouldn't think one small hotel in a small town would be able to support a car habit like that. I know tourism is good here—"

"But he'd have to have more than one hotel," Robert said.

"Ooo. I just thought of something. The person who ran over me doesn't necessarily have to own a white car. It could've been a rented car. Or even a borrowed car."

"Good point." Robert scribbled on the yellow tablet and studied the notes.

"Sylvia Cornelius lifts weights. So she'd have the strength to put such deep rope marks on Mr. Tankersly's neck."

"She was involved with Derek a couple of years back. She worked for him when he first moved here, probably just to be near him."

"She obviously still has some income, but doesn't work," Toni said.

"That gives her and Derek something in common, because even though he works, he obviously has an income

105

from other sources than the hotel. But Sheriff Braxton says she was at home when Jake was nearly murdered."

"Did anybody see her there?" Toni asked, trying to remember if she'd seen Sylvia at home before she went to the clinic. But she hadn't noticed.

"No. Jeff was out playing baseball with some of his friends. But Sylvia's at home at that time every day, so it's hardly a debatable alibi."

"Okay. Derek was in Mr. Tankersly's room about the time the ventilator was unplugged."

"He probably lied to the RN about who he was," Robert said.

"What do you mean probably? I thought Sheriff Braxton was supposed to call the RN to verify Barbara's story."

"Oh yeah, I forgot to tell you. Sheriff Braxton said the nurse was mugged in the hospital parking lot last night on the way to his car."

"Mugged?" Toni asked, thinking of how she walked through that same parking lot without a trace of fear.

"Yeah. And he died. Somebody shot him in the head."

"How awful!" she said.

"Yeah. The hospital is in an uproar. They're hiring more security and everything."

"So we can't disprove Derek's story."

"Right. But we still don't have a motive for him."

"Unless Mr. Tankersly knew something he shouldn't have, which is very likely because of the domino meeting every day. He could have stuck his nose into something without realizing it," Toni said.

"Right. Now, let's see. Somebody's trying to scare you. And Derek was at the hospital the night the tape showed up in your car."

"And besides that, the person has used two toy cars, a dummy, and a . . ." Toni broke off and shivered, " . . .a snake."

106

Robert looked at her, concern wrinkling his brow. "You okay?"

Toni nodded. "I think so."

Their faces were within inches of touching. And the same electricity which sprang between them at unexpected intervals picked that moment to make another appearance. A thrill surged through Toni's chest, leaving chill bumps and blazes in its path. The flickering firelight reflected in Robert's serious eyes. And his gaze wandered to her lips.

Toni hoped he wouldn't kiss her. And at the same time she hoped he would. If they became too involved, wouldn't that upset Bobby? But if they didn't become involved, wouldn't that upset her? Toni couldn't deny the fact that he'd really been the reason she'd gone shopping today.

Robert's face inched toward hers. Then he hesitated. The same conflict warring inside Toni was evident in his churning eyes. But that didn't stop him from moving toward her lips again.

Toni inhaled. "You said earlier today that Frank hates Jake, so he's got a good motive," she rushed, never taking her gaze from Robert's.

He blinked. "Nice sidestep," he mumbled, smiling in defeat.

Toni stood and walked across the room, her cheeks growing warm despite her wish for them not to. Why had she broken the moment? Hadn't she been longing for Robert to kiss her ever since he held her in his arms this afternoon? Yes. But that kiss would lead to a deeper level in their "iffy" relationship. And Toni couldn't risk getting hurt when Robert might be forced to choose between her and Bobby. Toni knew Bobby would win hands down.

Robert must have sensed her uneasiness for he went back to his business-like manner of clipping off clues in a strained voice. "Frank hates Jake and has a good motive, but he also has a good alibi. So do Barbara, Doug, and Gordon.

107

And Braxton says nobody in that family can afford to hire a killer because they don't have that kind of money. I don't think it was a job someone was hired to do, anyway."

"Why not?" she said, sitting on the edge of the blue sofa.

"Too unprofessional. I'm not saying a hit man can't mess up. But I think he'd have made sure Jacob was dead." Robert raked his hand through his dark hair in a jerking motion as if he were frustrated, but Toni couldn't tell if the frustration stemmed from the case or her recent retreat.

"Aunt Marge says Mr. Tankersly has several million dollars locked safely away in some bank somewhere. But he won't let anybody touch it." Toni scooted back on the couch.

"Whoa!" Robert said, staring at Toni with widened eyes.

"I was shocked too."

"Dogies! The sheriff said he had a lot, but I didn't imagine it was that much."

"Aunt Marge said it's old family money—gold money. Mr. Tankersly's father owned part of a mountain where gold was found, and to quote Aunt Marge again, he seems to think his children should make it on their own without his help. Frank and Barbara are doing okay financially. Doug isn't."

"Strike one up for Doug," Robert said. "Another good motive." He made a note on the pad.

"Yeah, but—"

"No evidence," Robert finished. "And he has an alibi."

Toni watched the fire. As silence stretched between them, she relived the moment that snake lunged out at her. Toni cringed, wishing the threats would stop, wishing she could put a stop to them herself. Then she cringed again with the thought of dying in that creep's arms.

"I'm fighting the urge to strangle whoever put that snake in my house."

"I know how you feel," Robert said. "I still want to strangle Wayne Freeman. And I think I would if I were given half the chance." An angry inferno raged in Robert's eyes.

The force of his bitterness hit Toni anew. What would it do to him if he hung on to it too long? Toni knew where she'd been headed. She'd seen it too many times in her older patients' eyes. Life had dealt them a few hard blows, and they'd carried around a bitter attitude until it became etched in their faces like a stone carving. It stared out of their eyes, disapproving of everyone and everything.

"Robert . . ." she said tentatively. "I don't really think I should want to strangle the man, though. That's why I'm fighting it."

"I stopped fighting it a long time ago," he growled. "I can't get Wayne's smug face out of my mind. He sat by at the trial, watching me go down like a drowning man, watching Bobby's life erupt around him."

Robert's gaze met Toni's. "Like I said, I've quit trying to stop the anger. It's here. It's part of me. It's the way it is." He pointed to his chest.

"But it doesn't have to be that way." Sensing she was pushing it to say as much as she had, Toni didn't say any more.

"I know." Heavy silence filled the room, the mantle clock's steady ticking the only noise.

Finally Robert patted the floor next to him and smiled, the bitterness retreating from his face like the fingers of a fog which never completely leave. "Come back here and sit down. We've got some clues to look over."

Toni hardly trusted herself that close to him. If he tried to kiss her again, she just might—

"You won't have to sidestep this time." He raised his hand, an impish grin playing on his lips, in his eyes. "Scout's honor."

Toni looked at the floor and bit her lip. "I'm sorry, it's just that, well—"

"You didn't want to kiss me. That's fine—"

"No, it isn't that."

"Oh, so you did want to kiss me," he teased, his eyes sparkling with male speculation.

"I didn't say that either."

"What are you trying to say?"

"I just don't want to start something that, well. . ."

"It's Bobby, isn't it?"

Toni exhaled. "You know he doesn't like me."

"No, not right now. But I bet he will eventually."

"How do you know?"

"Because I like you." He put the note pad aside and walked toward Toni, settling beside her on the couch. "And Bobby and I have always shared the same taste." Placing an arm around her, Robert pulled her closer.

Her heart kicking into overtime, Toni toyed with one of the fuchsia buttons on his shirt. "That might work with pizza, or, or ice cream, but it doesn't necessarily apply to people," she stammered.

Robert tilted up her chin to stare into her eyes. "It will this time . . ." His lips brushed hers in a soft caress. ". . . I hope," he whispered against her lips before the caress deepened.

Kissing Robert was like skydiving, or skiing down a dangerous mountain, or jumping into a deep, warm pool. Once you did it, there was no turning back. And the powerful jolt moving in her midsection told Toni she'd never be the same.

Robert lifted his head, his eyes gleaming behind narrow slits, his breathing not as steady as it should be.

Toni swallowed.

Wow. Double Wow.

CHAPTER 13

"It can't be," Toni mumbled to herself three days later as she stared into Tweety Bird's cage. A blue green parakeet stared back at her. But it *wasn't* Tweety Bird. And a white, toy car lay in the bottom of the bird's cage. A message. Letting Toni know her bird had been kidnapped.

Toni's mouth went dry. The white car had turned into a symbol of terror for the person harassing her. But why would he take her bird and leave another one? So far all the messages had been threatening. But stealing her bird wasn't what Toni would classify as a threat.

Not unless the harasser simply wanted you to know he had been in your house.

Toni's hands shook as she walked through her home, wondering how the person had entered. None of the windows were broken. None of them showed signs of forced entry. Her front door was locked when she came home from work only a few minutes ago. What about the back door?

Toni rushed through the kitchen to twist the back door's metal knob. It turned with ease. Her heart jumped into her throat and pounded like a judge's gavel punctuating a death sentence. She vividly remembered locking the door this morning before she left to take her car to the shop.

Toni pulled it open to examine the frame for signs of forced entry. But her gaze fell on something which answered her unasked question. A big, overturned stone lay in the flower bed right next to her back steps. The stone hadn't been overturned this morning. Her back door key hadn't been gone this morning, either.

Toni's legs trembled, her knee aching as she leaned against the door for support. She'd left the key there for Robert yesterday when he came to fix her living room window, and she'd forgotten to retrieve it. Someone knew the key was there. Someone had watched her and—

Had he seen Toni walk home from work? Did he know she had no car? Hot fury churned in her stomach as she slammed the door, turning the lock with trembling fingers. She had to call Robert.

"I'm callin' Sheriff Braxton," Robert said as soon as he'd examined the bird and car.

Toni watched as Robert dialed the number and wondered why she hadn't called the sheriff first instead of Robert. She hadn't even thought about it. Toni had been too busy wishing she could say a word or two to the person who took her pet. Where was Tweety Bird?

"It's just a stupid ol' bird," Bobby said as he stared into the cage, his hands stuffed into the back pockets of his blue jeans.

Just a stupid ol' bird? Toni remembered his similar comment three days ago about the snake, and it took more willpower this time for her to keep her mouth shut.

He turned his dark brown gaze to Toni. "Are you going

to move?" he asked with thinly disguised hope tainting his words.

"I—"

"No. She isn't," Robert said from behind her.

Toni looked over her shoulder. "How do you know?"

"I know you," he said, an arrogant tilt to his chin.

"Oh you do, do you?" One kiss, and the man thought he knew everything about her. She pushed up the sleeves of her peach cotton shirt.

"You don't run."

"And how do you know that?"

One corner of his mouth tilted. "Too stubborn." He chuckled.

Toni's mouth fell open. "Stubborn! Listen here, Mister—"

The sheriff's knock stopped her words.

After a routine examination resulting in another case of no fingerprints, the sheriff left, taking the white car with him, and leaving behind news that Mr. Tankersly had a bad night. Toni knew the old man teetered on the brink of life and death. She'd made Sheriff Braxton leave the bird. She felt sorry for the little creature who, except for his slightly bluer tint, looked almost just like Tweety Bird. Even though the bird had been put there to scare her, it acted more terrified than Toni did.

"I'm going to change your locks," Robert said as soon as the door closed behind the sheriff. "And I'm adding deadbolts. I don't care if it takes me till midnight."

"Thanks," Toni muttered.

But it didn't take Robert until midnight, and four hours later Toni had new, lockable knobs as well as deadbolt locks on her front and back doors.

During that time Bobby had fetched a few things for Robert. But he'd also spent a lot of time in Robert's pickup, refusing Toni's offer of a video and some microwave popcorn.

113

Munching the buttery popcorn he'd rejected, Toni watched Bobby from the front window as Robert cleaned up the wood shavings around the doors. Bobby had been reading, but he put down his book to concentrate on something in the truck's seat.

Toni's heart went out to the little boy who was nothing more than a miniature of the man who filled her dreams. He'd suffered through a lot of pain early in life. Toni hoped it didn't scar him permanently. A strong maternal instinct surged through her heart, leaving waves of compassion and unfulfilled longing in its wake. Frustration followed. Would Bobby let her get close enough to help?

"He's a good lookin' boy," Robert mumbled behind her.

"Sure is. I wish . . ." Toni sighed.

"I know," Robert said, placing his hands on her shoulders and turning her to face him. "He'll come around."

"I hope," Toni added just as Robert had Saturday evening.

Robert inhaled. "Me too."

"Want some popcorn?"

"Nah. I don't really care for that microwave stuff. When I eat popcorn, I like it from an air popper, lightly salted."

"Yuck."

"It's better for you that way. This stuff is full of fat and sodium and—"

"Here you go again, sounding like—"

"My mother." Robert shook his head.

"Actually, I was going to say Uncle Phil." Chuckling, Toni set the popcorn bag on the wicker table next to the window and dusted the salt off her fingers. "You'd make somebody a good housewife."

"I know." Robert rolled his eyes. "And sometimes it *really* bothers me."

"Oh well, maybe not a wife—but you'd for sure make somebody a good—" Toni stopped before she said "husband" but couldn't think of another word. As the silence

114

stretched between them, Toni considered biting her tongue in half. Her mouth seemed to have a mind of its own when she was with Robert.

His eyes glittering with laughter, Robert raised one eyebrow. "I'll make somebody a good what?"

"Um . . ." Toni peered past his shoulder to her breakfast bar, knowing there was only one face-saving way out of this predicament—change the subject. "Um . . . I think it would be a good idea if you didn't mention this—this thing with Tweety Bird to Aunt Marge and Uncle Phil. It'll just make them worry. Then they'll call my parents, and they'll worry."

"You know you really are good at changing the subject at the most interestin' times."

Biting her bottom lip, Toni tried hard not to smile. "You learn to develop that skill around Uncle Phil. And I'm serious about not telling him."

Robert sighed with exaggerated resignation. "Okay, the subject's officially changed. And I know they'll worry, but that just means they care about you."

"I know, but—"

"I won't push it," he said looking at the ruby pendant lying against Toni's peach shirt. "That another one of your grandmother's pieces?" he asked.

Toni fingered the unique, flower-shaped cluster. "Yes. It's my favorite."

"Pretty," he muttered, "like you." Robert pulled Toni into his arms, enveloping her in the warmth of his sandalwood smell. "Like your hair . . . what color do you call it?" he asked, stroking the hair at the nape of her neck.

Toni swallowed, reveling in the rush of heat radiating from his touch. "Strawberry blond."

"I like strawberries."

"I like you."

"Mmm. This feels good."

115

It feels right, Toni thought. She'd always questioned those people who said they knew when they'd met the right person at first sight or closely thereafter. Toni was beginning to doubt those reservations. Not that she and Robert had built a strong enough relationship to even be thinking in that direction, but the fact remained that next to Robert was the place she wished to stay.

"I'm worried about you," he whispered.

"Me too. And I'm scared." Toni's heart quivered with the sound of warm concern in his voice.

"If it's okay with you, I'm going to order some new locks for your windows and install them. Yours are still sturdy, but they're old. And I don't want to take any chances."

"Sounds good to me. Just remember to send me the bill. I still owe you for the window, and now the door locks."

"No bill. It's on the house," Robert said, easing back.

"I can't let you do that—"

" 'Course not. I'm gonna do it whether you let me or not." He winked.

Smiling, Toni narrowed her eyes. *"Now* who's stubborn? I owe you money, and I'm going to pay you."

"You've already paid me. Don't you know that smile's worth a million bucks? It's like sunshine."

Toni held her breath as Robert brushed the corner of her mouth with his thumb, then with his lips.

"Mmm. This could be hazardous to your health," he mumbled, a derisive smile tilting his mouth.

Or to your heart, Toni thought.

"I meant to ask you earlier and forgot—where's your car?" he asked, his voice low and caring as if he'd just told her he loved her.

"Um . . ." Toni couldn't think straight with him this close, with that look in his eyes, with her heart melting like warm honey. ". . . um, it's got an electrical problem. So I took it to the shop this morning and walked home from work."

"You walked home? Why didn't you call me, or get your uncle or aunt to give you a ride?"

"I've been walking more, and running some too. It's good for my knee. Keeps it from getting stiff."

"You need to be careful," he growled. "You don't need to be out—"

"Dad?" Bobby called, pushing open the front door.

Toni jumped away from Robert, feeling as if she'd been caught in a heinous crime. Bobby's accusing eyes didn't help matters. And Toni knew her guilty blush only added to Bobby's accusation.

"What did you want, son?" Robert asked, draping an arm around Toni's shoulders. "Don't pull away. He's going to have to get used to it," he whispered.

Bobby raised his hands, and a large, brownish-green bullfrog peered at them from across Bobby's fingers. Struggling against the boy's grip, his legs hung out from the bottom of Bobby's fists. "My frog, he . . ." Bobby exhaled. "Your truck seat's wet."

"Oh no," Robert groaned, rubbing his eyes. "You know I just had my interior cleaned. And I told you not to bring any more frogs in my truck anyway."

"Well . . . I didn't mean to. But I borrowed him from Sam today, and he escaped from my duffel bag on the way home this afternoon."

"He spent the night with Sam last night," Robert said, filling Toni in on the details.

"I didn't know he wasn't in my duffel bag till I got home, but I thought maybe he escaped in the house. Then I was sitting out there, and he came crawlin' out from under the seat. I didn't mean for him to get in your truck."

Toni bit her bottom lip and ducked her head to stop the laughter. But Bobby yelled, and Toni looked back up. The frog jumped from Bobby's grip, and hopped across the living room floor in amphibian madness.

"Bob-by!" Robert exclaimed, dropping to his knees and making a grab for the bullfrog. But it hopped over his hands, smiling in smug victory as it continued his journey across the floor.

Toni doubled over in laughter.

Bobby ran in front of the frog, dropping to his knees to try to cut off the brown-green creature. But the frog outsmarted Bobby and took a sharp right hop, landing under the couch.

"Are you going to help or just stand there and laugh?" Robert asked through a chuckle. He stuck his hand under the sofa's edge.

But the frog was already crawling out the back. Toni bent to catch him, scooping his palpitating body into her hands. "I got him," she yelled in victory.

Shutting his eyes, Robert shook his head and stood. "I can't believe this. Where'd Sam get a frog this size?"

Bobby stood up. "From his cousin in Louisiana. He borrowed him for a while."

Toni snickered.

Bobby peered at Toni with disappointment clouding his face. "You mean you aren't afraid of frogs?"

Toni handed him the bullfrog, wondering just how much of an "accident" this escapade had been. "No. Frogs are harmless."

"Do you have a couple of towels I could borrow?" Robert asked. "I'll wash 'em before I bring 'em back." He tugged on his denim shirt's collar in agitation.

Nodding, Toni went to the kitchen, stifling a giggle.

"This is not funny," Robert growled, taking the dish towels from her. "I just had my interior cleaned."

Toni suppressed the laughter, feeling like a volcano waiting to explode.

"You lock your doors tight tonight, you hear?"

"Yes," Toni said through a giant smile.

Robert's lips twitched. "I'll remember this one day," he said over his shoulder as he walked toward Bobby. "I told you no more frogs in the truck, Bobby—last week. Now look what's happened. . . ." He shut the door.

Chuckling, Toni watched the two of them walk across her lawn. She could just imagine the loads and loads of laundry Robert must do to keep up with Bobby. Toni didn't like to do her own laundry, much less—

She blinked. What was she thinking? Robert's laundry wasn't her concern. Why should she care how much laundry he did?

As Robert backed his truck out of her driveway and started down the road, a movement across the street caught Toni's attention.

She drew her breath in surprise. Derek stood on Sylvia's porch, stuffing something under his tan leather jacket. Sylvia was close to him, a worried frown marring her brow.

Derek pulled her into his arms, placing a gentle kiss on her forehead. He seemed to be talking to her. Though Toni couldn't hear the words, she could tell from Derek's expression and the way he lightly touched Sylvia's cheek that he wanted to soothe her. But Sylvia's anxious look showed signs of definite worry.

Toni subconsciously strained her ears as if she could hear Sylvia and Derek from inside her house. What was going on? Toni thought Robert said Sylvia and Derek were no longer seeing each other. But from the kiss Derek just placed on Sylvia's waiting lips, Toni would assume they were back together.

Derek walked toward the red Mercedes sitting in Sylvia's driveway while Sylvia leaned against her yellow porch railing and watched him go.

"Don't worry," Derek mouthed before sliding into his car and driving away.

CHAPTER 14

Don't worry about what? What was going on here?
At two a.m. Toni flopped over onto her stomach
for the sixth time. The peach comforter, already in
a state of mass confusion, tangled around her legs. Sleep
was a forgotten luxury, replaced by churning thoughts and
the smell of freshly washed sheets.

She couldn't stop thinking about Robert Hooper for one
thing. And for another thing, Toni kept wondering if Derek
was the one who tried to kill Mr. Tankersly and who was
trying to scare her.

Toni had called Sheriff Braxton, but news of Sylvia and
Derek's reconciliation was no news to him. The grapevine
had already supplied him with that detail. Yet he had no
idea why Sylvia should be worried.

Toni rolled onto her back. She'd thought about calling
Robert and discussing this latest development, but hadn't.
She didn't want to push their relationship any faster than it

was already going. After every time she made contact with the man, she felt like she'd been through an emotional tornado.

Could they be falling in love? *Oh Rats! I don't know. I've never done it before.* With that thought, Toni finally drifted into a fitful sleep.

But a far-away bumping penetrated Toni's sleep. Was the bumping part of a dream, or was it real? The noise repeated itself, and a rasping followed.

Toni rose to the twilight state where reality merges with the dream world. The noise grew louder. But she was so groggy, and her nose—cold. Pulling her hand from its warm spot under the cover, Toni rubbed her nose. Frigid air sucked the warmth from her hand.

Why is it so cold in here?

The noise from her dream moved to the end of her bed. But now it sounded like tiny pieces of metal clinking together.

It wasn't a dream! Every cell in her body exploded in a full awakening. Her eyes flew open. The first thing Toni saw was the filmy, beige window sheers billowing away from the window as night air filled the room. She hadn't left the window open!

A shadow moved at the end of her bed. Toni jerked her gaze toward it. A man stood at her dresser, dumping the contents of her jewelry box into some kind of bag. It was too dark to see much.

Toni's stomach turned to jelly, then knotted and unknotted in aching contractions. *Oh no! Not Grandma's jewelry!*

The hazy moonlight outlined the intruder who systematically removed one drawer after another, emptying their contents as if the jewelry were from a gum ball machine.

Toni panted in horror, struggling to keep quiet. Her arms and legs shook uncontrollably. What could she do? Did he have a gun? He must not know she lay only a few feet away, because he wasn't trying to hold down the noise.

121

The car. She'd left it at the shop.

He must think she wasn't home. If Toni moved, he'd spot her. And he might shoot her. But if she didn't move or do something to stop him, he'd crawl back out the window and carry away a bag full of irreplaceable memories.

The shaking extended from Toni's arms and legs to her lips. Sweat covered her whole body, but she shivered at the same time.

He gripped the last drawer.

Do something!

The brass lamp—sitting on the night stand. If Toni could pick it up at its base without him seeing her, she could trip the robber, whack him over the head, tie him up in the sheets, and call the sheriff.

Would it work? *It has to. It's my only choice.*

Breathing in shallow gasps, Toni bit her lips together until they went numb, squinted her eyes, and willed herself to inch for the bed's edge like a turtle in slow motion. *Please God, don't let him see me.*

Centimeter by centimeter, she drew closer to her goal, her legs tingling with the feel of skin on sheets. Holding her breath, she scooted one last time, balancing on the edge of the mattress. Toni felt as if she were teetering on an unsteady rope bridge hanging over a gaping canyon.

Nervously, she glanced to the end of her bed. The burglar tied the cloth bag into a knot at the top. Toni peered back at the lamp.

Go for it!

She leaned just a fraction further, stretching for the lamp. But that fraction knocked her off balance, and Toni lost her grip. Her attempts to stay on the bed failed, and Toni plummeted to the hardwood floor.

Throwing her hands out, she tried to soften the impact of flesh on wood. Toni's hands hit first, but her right knee landed next. Excruciating pain ravaged up her thigh and down her shin. And a low groan forced its way past her lips.

"Who's there?" a gravelly voice asked.

Toni licked her lips. Almost whimpering in dread, she gripped her throbbing knee. *I don't want to die. I'm too young to die. I want a husband and children—and a life.*

The robber's shadow crossed her feet. Toni shrank from it, trying to scoot under the bed. Maybe he wouldn't see her if she could just get under the—

"Stop!"

Toni went rigid. And the well-oiled, cold-metal sound of a gun being cocked in slow motion nearly stopped her heart. Looking up, She stared into the end of a revolver. The moonlight reflected off its black, evil contours, sending chills through Toni's body.

"This is all your fault," he growled. "You know that, don't you?"

Toni tore her gaze from the gun and focused on its owner. A gray overcoat wrapped his body. A blood-red ski mask stretched over his face.

"Wh-what are you talking about?" Toni croaked in a voice she didn't recognize. How could his robbing her be her fault? Was he crazy?

His lips curled away from dingy teeth which gaped through the ski mask's mouth hole. "If you hadn't been jogging, I wouldn't have hit you. And I wouldn't have to pay. Well, I'm tired of paying. It's your turn now." He shook the revolver at her, his eyes glittering in dark, wicked slits.

Toni's limbs trembled anew. She stared at the very man responsible for almost killing her two years ago.

But what was he talking about? *He* had to pay. Pay what? She was the one paying. For nothing! Just like Robert. Just like Jacob Tankersly. Toni was a victim of someone else's sordid nature.

Gritting her teeth, she took a slow, cleansing, calming

breath. She wouldn't go down without a fight. "Get out of my house," Toni hissed. "Get out of my house!" *Greater is He that is in me—*

"Have you forgotten?" The man pointed the gun at her face. "I'm the one with the gun."

He pulled the trigger.

Screaming, Toni buried herself against the bed, the bullet whizzing past her ear like a death missile. Her stomach spewed acid as the room went in and out of focus. "God, save me," she whispered.

He laughed maliciously. "Praying won't help you. I'm getting used to killing people. And you might not be as lucky as Tankersly."

Toni licked her lips and forced down a whimper, her bravado evaporating as fast as that bullet had left its chamber. "Look, I don't want to cause any problems. Why don't you take the jewelry and . . . and leave."

He lowered the gun at her face, shut his left eye in aim, and pulled the hammer back with a click.

This is it. I'm going to die. For one breathless minute Toni stared into the end of the revolver like a helpless animal at the mercy of a cruel hunter.

He lifted the gun off her. "Maybe I won't kill you after all. You're too pretty to die." His voice held a twisted caress, and Toni's stomach churned with a new kind of fear. "Besides . . . I didn't plan another murder. Just this." He raised the cloth bag.

"But stay out of my way. Or next time . . ." he turned for the window, " . . . I'll do to you what you did to my snake." With that, he slithered out the window.

A warm rush flooded Toni's face, her eyes blurring with thankful tears as she gulped for air. She collapsed against the floor. A sob tore through her. *Thank God I'm alive.*

But her moment of relief lasted only seconds. Toni looked toward the window, opened wide. He could change

124

his mind and come back in. Forcing her throbbing right knee to cooperate, Toni crawled across the room, rose up on her good knee and slammed the window down. With trembling fingers she tried to relock it, only to discover he'd broken the lock, leaving it useless.

Biting her shaking bottom lip, Toni hobbled for the phone on her night stand. She had to call Sheriff Braxton.

She'd barely tied her yellow, terry cloth robe around her before the sheriff pounded on the door. She glanced toward the empty jewelry box, searching in vain for some sign of sparkle. But every last piece was gone. Her heart ached as if she'd lost her best friend—her best memories.

Gritting her teeth until her jaw throbbed almost as bad as her knee, Toni hobbled up the hall to let the sheriff in. The way he was pounding on the door, Toni was sure he'd break it down before she got to it.

But when she opened the door, Sheriff Braxton wasn't standing there. Robert was. He towered in the doorway, grasping the frame as if he were ready to tear it down.

"Robert! What—"

He pushed past her. "Where'd he break in?" he asked, whipping a gun from his waistband.

"It's the window in my bedroom. But how—"

"The one facing the back of the house or the side?"

"The back. Did Sheriff Brax—"

"You stay put," he said, leveling a gaze on her that dared her to do otherwise.

"I'm fine. Thanks for asking," Toni said sarcastically.

Robert cocked one eyebrow. "I can see that," he clipped, rushing for the door.

Frowning, Toni crossed her trembling arms and leaned against the wall for support. Robert Hooper could really get on her nerves sometimes. And he'd picked the wrong time to act high-handed. Toni stared at the parakeet's covered cage and wondered where Tweety Bird was, if he were still alive.

In a few minutes, Robert stomped through the kitchen. "Nothin'."

Toni took a deep, quivering breath and nodded. "I figured he'd be gone."

Robert neared her, concern filling his eyes. "Are you sure you're all right?" He stuffed the gun back into his waistband.

"No."

"Ah, Toni," he said, crushing her to him.

Toni relaxed into his warm safety, the irritation draining away as his body heat soothed her nerves.

"I'm—I'm sorry I had to go chasing 'round your backyard before—this. But if I'd stopped—and—well . . . I wouldn't have gone out there."

"I understand." She inhaled his clean, soapy scent. "I was so scared. I thought I was going to die." Toni snuggled closer to him, tightening her arms around his midsection. Aunt Marge's saying Toni needed a husband held an appealing ring at this moment.

"I nearly had a heart attack when Sheriff Braxton called."

"Why did he call you?" She looked up at Robert. "Does he know about . . ."

"About us?" A teasing light shone in Robert's eyes as he tucked a strand of hair behind her ear.

Toni lowered her gaze to the opening of his wrong-side-out olive-colored sweater. Us. It sounded so . . . together.

Robert stroked her cheek. "I don't think so. He knows I've been keeping an eye on you. And he has this idea I'm going to start workin' with him. He won't take no for an answer. I think this is his way of forcing me into it. He wants me to run for sheriff in the fall."

"I'm glad he picked tonight to force you into it." It felt so good to have someone . . . special, someone to share her pain.

"I'm glad too."

"Where's Bobby?" she asked, wondering about him for the first time.

"He's asleep in the truck. I didn't want to leave him at home, and I didn't want to bring him in here either because I didn't know what might happen."

The front door swept open, and someone cleared his throat.

CHAPTER 15

No wonder I got such good reports from the police department in Dallas, Robert. If you treated all the female victims like this, you were probably the most favored law officer around," Sheriff Braxton said.

Toni disengaged herself from Robert's embrace, but he kept one arm firmly around her shoulders.

The sheriff pushed past them, closing the door as he went, and throwing Robert a conspiring glance.

"Just doin' my job, Sheriff," Robert said.

"Yeah." Sheriff Braxton looked at Toni. "You wanta show me the jewelry box and where he broke in?"

Toni inhaled. "Sure. It was in my bedroom."

"Do you have an extra room I could put Bobby in till I go back home?" Robert asked. "I don't want to leave him out in the truck."

Toni nodded, thinking what a good father Robert was. And he obviously thought the world revolved around his son. She helped him get the drowsy Bobby settled, then they joined the sheriff in her bedroom.

Toni hated having to face that empty jewelry box. Those precious stones meant so much to her. She felt as if the robber had emptied a section of her heart, too.

"I take it you didn't see any sign of the guy, Sheriff?" Robert asked.

"Nah. I parked my car down the street and covered the whole block on foot. But he was already gone."

Toni sank to the edge of her bed and watched Robert and the sheriff look over her dresser and window. Then Robert went out to his truck and came back with a hammer and two long nails.

He nailed the window shut and turned to face her. "That'll have to do till I get the locks on."

She gripped her hands together, trying to suppress the urge to punch that man in the nose—whoever he was. Wasn't everything else he'd done enough?

"Okay, Doc," Sheriff Braxton said after he'd taken photos inside and outside and dusted for prints. "I couldn't find the bullet out there. It went right through your wall, though. So I know it's gotta be in your yard somewhere. Findin' it's a different matter. I'm coming back tomorrow during the daylight and see if I have any better luck. But I need you to tell me everything that happened, everything he said. Maybe if I sleep on it, I'll come up with something."

Toni balled her hands until her fingernails ate into her palms. "I woke up with him emptying the jewelry into a cloth bag of some kind—maybe a pillowcase. But there was only the moonlight, so I really couldn't tell. Anyway, I decided to try and get the lamp and hit him over the head with it."

"You what?" Robert blurted.

"Well, I couldn't just . . . just let him get away with all that jewelry."

129

"Let her finish, son."

Toni inhaled. "So I tried to get the lamp, but it was too far away. And that's when I fell out of bed and hit my knee."

"You hit your knee?" Robert asked with concern. "Is that why you're limping?"

Clearing his throat, Braxton gave Robert a pointed look.

"Yes," Toni said. "And that's when he knew I was in the room. I think he thought I wasn't home since my car isn't in the driveway."

Toni looked at Sheriff Braxton. "It's at the shop. Anyway, he told me it was my fault he was robbing me because if I hadn't been jogging two years ago, he wouldn't have hit me."

"Whoa," Robert said. "The man who broke in here is the man who ran over you?"

"That's what he said. And he told me he was having to pay, and now it's my turn to pay."

"Pay what?" Sheriff Braxton asked.

Toni shrugged. "I don't know. And then, I told him to get out of my house. And that's when—"

"Wait a minute," Robert said. "He's the one with the gun, and *you* told *him* to get out of your house?"

Sheriff Braxton raised his hands in a huff.

"I got a little—angry there for a second."

"I guess that's when he shot at you?" Robert asked.

"Yes," Toni answered in a quaking voice. An image of a black revolver flashed into her mind. "Interferers die" pulsed through her brain. She closed her eyes, trying to dissolve the picture and remove the words.

But a white car, reeling toward her took the revolver's place. The dummy followed, then the snake, then Tweety Bird, wherever he was. And the demon-like words repeated themselves over and over again. "Interferers die. Interferers die. And you'll die in my arms."

130

The bed gave way beneath her, and Robert draped an arm around her shoulders.

Opening her eyes, Toni took a cleansing breath, trying to wash away the haunting voice. "After he shot at me, he said he was getting used to killing people. And that I might not be as lucky as Tankersly."

"Murder number one," Robert muttered, looking up at the sheriff.

"Do you think ol' Jake knew he was number one in a series of murders?" Sheriff Braxton asked.

"I don't know," Robert said. "I wonder if that's what he meant? Or something else . . ."

"I guess this rules Sylvia out," Sheriff Braxton said, his eyes narrowed. "Seein' as the person who broke in here was a man. Unless she's in cahoots with Derek."

"Right," Robert said. "And can we safely assume that all the other threats to Toni are by the same person?"

"It would make sense," Sheriff Braxton said, "with all those white cars that keep turning up."

"I forgot something," Toni said. "He said if I got in his way, he'd do to me what I did to his snake."

"I chopped off its head," Robert said.

"So it is the same one," Sheriff Braxton mumbled, rubbing his head.

"How did he know I chopped off the snake's head, though?"

"He's watching," Toni said, crossing her arms and rubbing her forearms.

"Who all knows you have that jewelry?" the sheriff asked.

"Anybody could know. I wear it all the time."

"How much was it worth, Toni?" Robert asked.

Toni swallowed. "The insurance appraisal said eighty-five thousand."

Sheriff Braxton whistled.

"But I don't care about the money." Toni looked up at Robert. "It's the memories," she whispered.

"I know," Robert mumbled.

"That's true, Doc. But I'm glad it was insured, all the same."

"I was going to order a safe. My other house had one built in. I could kick myself for not doing it before, but I've been so distracted with everything else that's happened. . . ." Toni raised her hand in frustration.

Robert shook his head. "And I thought Ouray was going to be a nice, quiet place to raise my son."

"It used to be," Sheriff Braxton growled. "I don't know what's gotten into people. I haven't had this many crimes in I don't know when. It didn't start till you moved here." He looked at Toni. "Do you have a curse on you I should know about?" His eyes glittered. "Nah. The only curse I see has something to do with Cupid."

Toni bit her bottom lip. So much for privacy. By tomorrow noon everybody in Ouray would know the new doctor was seen in the arms of the new handyman.

But a glance to her dresser banished Toni's privacy worries and doubled her sense of loss and violation. A dark cloud of sorrow spread through her. Toni's heart labored as her throat tightened. Grandma Weston cherished her beloved jewelry. Now it was gone. Gone. Just like Grandma.

A silent tear trickled down Toni's cheek. Ducking her head, she shrugged off Robert's arm and limped to the living room. Robert's and Sheriff Braxton's voices echoed in her ears, but she only heard a few words—"Sylvia," "Derek," and "back together." Pushing all thoughts of who was behind her dilemma out of her mind, Toni picked up Sylvester from his favorite corner on the couch and sat down with him in her lap.

One tear after another streamed down her cheeks as her

sense of loss increased. She heard the front door shut as if it were far, far away.

Robert sat beside her, and she glanced up at him. Compassion stirring in his eyes, he stroked her cheek. "I'm sorry this happened." Reaching out, he wrapped his arms around her, pulling her next to him.

New tears welling within her, she sniffled against his olive-colored sweater. "I'm sorry I'm crying like this, but Grandma's only been gone two months. I don't think I'm over that. And now this. . . ." Her voice cracked.

He stroked her hair and sighed. "We're not the most fortunate pair are we?"

Toni nodded and pressed a little closer to him. She'd always been so strong and so independent. It felt so nice to lean on someone else for a change. This could become a serious habit.

"I don't think it would be wise for you to try to go to work in the mornin'—this mornin'. You can't have had more than a few hours sleep. And it's already five after five." Robert pushed the hair away from her face.

Toni drew back and fumbled in her robe pocket for a tissue. "I have to. It's Uncle Phil's morning off, and he's going fishing with somebody down at Molas Lake."

"He's going fishin' with me, and I can wait till another time."

Toni dried her eyes. "No. I can't make him come in. He's worked here for so many years, always on call—including Saturdays and Sundays. He deserves some time off."

"He won't mind," Robert urged. "And besides, exactly how many hours of sleep did you get?"

Toni looked at him in doubt. She hadn't gone to sleep until three or so, and it was five now. She couldn't have slept more than an hour, maybe thirty minutes.

"How many?"

"About one, give or take." Toni looked across the room,

hoping Robert didn't suspect that he was partially to blame for her insomnia.

He grunted. "More than I got. But still not enough."

Toni darted her gaze back to him. His right brow arched as his lips twitched. So he hadn't been able to sleep either? *Serves him right.*

"Besides, I think this fishing trip Dr. Weston's conjured up is a thin excuse to try to persuade me to work for him," Robert said.

"We could use you. But what about Sheriff Braxton?"

Robert's eyes clouded and he looked past her. "I'm not ready for any of it," he growled.

"Oh."

Inhaling, he looked toward the ceiling. "Sorry. It's just so hard to . . ."

"To forgive?" Toni prompted, hoping she wasn't over-stepping the boundaries.

"Yeah," he said.

"I know. I've been there. Still am. It's almost as hard to maintain the forgiveness as it is to make the initial decision to forgive. But you'll pull through." Toni smiled at him. "I know you will."

Robert touched the corner of her mouth. "You know what that smile reminds me of? Sunshine. It's just like the sun on a summer day. It lights up the whole room. How could I not pull through with you smiling like that?"

Toni's emotions tilted like an unstable buoy on choppy waters, leaving her breathless. Every time she saw Robert, her feelings grew stronger and harder to ignore.

Robert stroked her cheek with the back of his fingers. "I almost had a heart attack when Sheriff Braxton called." He lowered his forehead to hers, slipping his arms around her, pulling her closer. "Mmm."

Toni's lips met Robert's halfway. Moments passed. Moments when Toni felt as important as the air Robert breathed. Moments which left her trembling and bemused.

Robert lifted his lips from hers, shifting his shaking hands from her shoulders to her face, and stroking her cheeks with his thumbs.

Wave after wave of happiness washed over Toni. Was that love flickering in the black depths of Robert's eyes?

With a sigh, Robert struggled to his feet and headed to the other side of the room. "Do you think you'll be all right by yourself now? I need to be gettin' Bobby home."

"I—I think so." Toni moved Sylvester to the couch and stood, taking a step toward Robert. "I need to start thinking about work anyway."

Robert raised his hand. "I want you to get some sleep. I'll call your uncle in the mornin'—in an hour or so—and tell him you won't be coming in."

Toni frowned. "But—"

"No." Robert stopped her in mid-protest. "I won't even hear it."

"I'm going to work," Toni snapped. She'd lost more than one night's sleep in her life, and she wasn't about to let some—some arrogant man tell her—

"No! You need some sleep. And I don't want you going in till you've had some."

Toni blinked, her stomach knotting with anger. "So what! Since when do you run my life? If you think you can come in here and, and kiss me a few times, and then have the right to order me around—"

"I'll make sure Sheriff Braxton doesn't bother you till after lunch," he clipped, turning to go get Bobby.

Toni stood with her arms crossed and watched Robert help Bobby to the front door. "You know, you really get on my nerves sometimes," she muttered.

"That makes two of us," he shot back, shutting the door behind him.

"Robert Hooper, you're the most bullheaded, stubborn,

bossy man I've ever met in my life," Toni mumbled as she checked the window locks. "And leave it to me to already be halfway in love with you."

Examining the last window behind her brass bed's headboard, Toni noticed a light flickering through her bushes, and the faint crunching of footsteps . . .

Her heart pounded so hard she felt it behind her eyes. Had the robber come back to finish her off?

Chapter 16

Robert brooded as he watched the coffee drip into the clear, glass pot. Sleep was out of the question. He'd drink a couple of cups of coffee, and maybe they'd take away the fogginess in his mind. Then when six rolled around, he'd call Phil Weston. He had thirty minutes to wait.

Something thudded in Bobby's room, sounding like a body being dumped out the window next to the kitchen. Robert's heart skipped a beat, and he rushed toward the room. Probably nothing but his imagination. He hoped. But after Toni's experience, Robert wasn't taking any chances.

He whipped open Bobby's bedroom door to find the twin bed empty. Robert's hands shook. He flipped on the light. A collection of mismatched socks, some baseball cards, and two pairs of underwear were mixed in with the sheets.

Incoherent thoughts bombarded Robert. *Where is Bobby?*

In the bathroom? In the closet?

"Bobby!" Robert called, running to the closet.

Empty.

"Bobby!" He rushed to the bathroom.

No Bobby.

Robert tore back into Bobby's room, noticing the open window for the first time, stopping to listen for the first time.

A low moan reached him from outside the window. Robert strode toward it and peered into the predawn shadows. Bobby lay on the ground, just outside the house.

"Bobby, what in heaven's name?"

"I think I sprained my ankle," he said in a tight, pain-filled voice.

"Hold it right there, Champ."

Five minutes later, Robert settled Bobby on the couch and took a look at the boy's ankle. "It isn't swelling," Robert muttered, "but it won't hurt to let Toni look at it."

"No!" Bobby said.

Robert blinked and stared at his son in surprise. Then his tired mind started clicking. "Why were you outside the window? It's five-thirty in the mornin'. I thought you were asleep."

Bobby looked across the room, refusing to meet Robert's gaze.

"Bobby?" Using his index finger, Robert tilted Bobby's chin, angling the boy's face in his direction. "Look at me. What's goin' on?" It all made sense, now. The socks. The underwear. The baseball cards. The duffel bag lying on the ground beside Bobby. Robert had been too shaken to put it all together.

Bobby's face might be directed to Robert, but he gazed downward shamefully.

"You were running away, weren't you?" Robert asked incredulously, remembering being a nine-year-old runaway

138

himself. His mom decided to fix spinach for supper, and Robert refused to eat it even if it meant hiding out at his best friend's until the threat was over. The anguish he'd caused his parents came back to haunt him.

"Answer me!"

"Yes, sir," Bobby said in a shaking voice.

"Why?"

"You know why!" Bobby cried. He gulped for air, his brown eyes challenging Robert. "You like her better than me!"

"Who?" Robert frowned in confusion, then it hit him. "You mean Toni?"

"Yeah!" Bobby's eyes filled with tears. "And I don't like her. And you don't care!"

"Ah, Bobby." Robert scrubbed his hand through his hair, wanting to pull it out. He'd been afraid of this from the very beginning. "I don't like her better than you. Don't you know, I love you, son. I'd never do anything—"

"But you love her more, don't you? I saw you kissin' her before we left her house. I know what it means when grownups kiss! I've seen Sam's mom and dad kiss. They're married. And I don't want us to marry her!"

Robert inhaled as Bobby's words punctured the room's pregnant silence. Bobby must have been spying on him and Toni this morning. Robert had known from the very first time he'd visited Toni Kirkpatrick that she'd be a threat to his vow never to disrupt Bobby's life again. But he'd talked himself into believing that Bobby would eventually grow to love Toni just as he found himself doing. It didn't look like that was going to happen.

Robert couldn't forfeit Bobby's happiness for his own selfish desires. The boy had already been through too much. Robert thought of all the letters Bobby had sent him in prison, of all the visits, of all the tears they'd shed. He couldn't do any more to hurt his son.

"We won't marry her," Robert whispered.

"Does that mean you won't go see her anymore?"

"Yes." Robert swallowed hard, hating the sound of that word and what it meant. But sometimes being a parent meant sacrificing what you wanted for what was best for your child.

Robert hugged his son. "I love you more than life." Taking the boy's shoulders in his hands, Robert looked right into his eyes. "And I don't want you to ever forget it."

A tear spilled from Bobby's eye. "Okay."

"And no more running away—for any reason. The next time, I'll tan your hide! Got it?"

"Yes, sir."

Robert wanted to shed a few tears of his own. He knew Toni could make him the happiest man alive. And being forced to break her heart was going to kill him. But that was the way things stood. Reality wasn't always neat and tidy with happy little endings. Not his reality, anyway.

"I'm going to put some ice on this ankle and let you stay on the couch till the clinic opens. It might be sprained."

"It already feels better," Bobby rushed.

"We'll let Dr. Weston decide that," Robert said.

CHAPTER 17

The footsteps drew nearer Toni's window. With quaking fingers, she clicked off the bedside lamp, plunging the room into darkness. The flashlight's beam seemed to glow brighter now, puncturing the bushes that grew head high on the side of Toni's house.

Fear paralyzing her, Toni panted. Cold sweat popped out along her upper lip. She had to move. She had to call Sheriff Brax—

Just outside the window, a dog barked and whined.

The noise startling her taunt nerves, Toni couldn't stop the compulsive scream.

"Dr. Kirkpatrick?" a woman called, the house walls muffling her voice. "Are you all right?"

Toni's pulse slowed in relief.

"He-hello?" she called back. "Wh-who's there?" Toni unlocked the window and raised it an inch.

"It's me, Sylvia Cornelius."

"What are you doing out there?" Toni asked, not too sure her relief was valid.

"I was taking Baby for a walk, and she got away from me."

"At five-thirty in the morning?"

"She woke me up, and I knew it was that or clean up the mess later." Sylvia hesitated. "What's been going on over here?"

Toni was reluctant to tell Sylvia about her intruder. What if Derek or she were involved? What if tracking down Baby was just an excuse for Sylvia to snoop around?

But Toni toyed with the idea of telling Sylvia anyway. Maybe her reaction to the news would give Toni a lead.

"Why don't you come around to the front porch?"

"Okay, but I can't come in. Derek's coming for breakfast at seven, and I need to get dressed and start cooking."

Toni walked to the front of her house. Apparently Derek and Sylvia had not only gotten back together, but were seeing quite a bit of each other. He'd just been over there last night.

Holding the squirming Cocker spaniel in one hand and a leash in the other, Sylvia walked onto Toni's porch. Her pale, round face showed signs of weariness and worry. She nervously tugged on her blue cardigan.

"So what happened? I saw the sheriff's car and Robert Hooper's pickup, and wondered . . ." she trailed off.

"I . . . had a burglar."

"A burglar?" Sylvia's blue eyes widened in what appeared to be genuine surprise.

Toni relaxed a bit.

"What did he take?"

"Some jewelry."

"Was it worth much?"

Toni swallowed. "Yes."

"And he just came right in on you?"

"Yes."

142

"I thought I heard a gunshot this morning about three, but decided I was imagining things. Did he . . ."

"Yes. He shot at me, but I don't think he really meant to kill me. Just scare me."

Sylvia's gaze slid from Toni's. "I . . . don't guess you could identify him?"

"I don't think so."

Some of the worry left Sylvia's face. "That's too bad," she said. "Did the sheriff find the bullet?"

"No. It went through my wall—" Toni cut herself off. Sylvia was asking some very detailed questions. Why?

Toni's phone rang. She glanced into the house.

"Well, you've got to go, and so do I," Sylvia said. "I'm really sorry to hear about the burglary. I think I might get Derek to make sure my window locks are all still good."

"Yeah, good idea," Toni said, wondering why Sylvia hadn't said door locks. It was as if she knew Toni's burglar had come through the window.

Toni narrowed her eyes. And Sylvia was wearing a blue sweater. Would it match the blue piece of fuzz the sheriff found on Toni's screen? She would definitely call Sheriff Braxton about this. The telephone rang for the third time, and locking the door behind her, Toni went to answer it.

"Robert just called," Uncle Phil said. "Are you all right?"

"I'm fine." Toni yawned.

"Well, listen, there's no need for you to come in today. I told Robert I'd take your place, and he and I could go fishing another time."

"No," Toni said, emphatically. "It's my turn to work by myself. You and Aunt Marge deserve some time together. Besides, you know I've worked without sleep before. And you've done the same."

"Heavenly day, Toni, somebody broke into your house, shot at you, and you haven't slept all night. Now lie down

143

and at least take a nap. If you want to come in this afternoon—"

"I'm coming in at seven-thirty when I was scheduled to
in the first place. You lie down and take a nap. It's your
day off."

"You're just as stubborn as my sister."

"That's what Dad says," Toni said, chuckling.

At seven-thirty-five the clinic door opened, and Toni
looked up from a quick bite of cold pizza and a gulp of
black coffee. Robert carried Bobby into the waiting room as
if he were a baby. Bobby wore one shoe, the other foot
donning only a sock.

Toni frowned. "What happened?"

His eyes widening, Robert stopped. "What are you doin'
here?"

"I told you I was coming in." Lifting her chin, Toni
straightened her lab coat's collar, and dared him with her
gaze to say anything more about it.

Robert inhaled in resignation. "Stubborn, stubborn, stubborn. . . . I don't guess Dr. Weston's in?" he asked tersely.

"No, why? You don't trust me with Bobby's problem?"
Toni matched his tone.

"It isn't that," he snapped, then looked at his son.

Bobby stared at Toni, a frown marring his brow.

"Just a minute," Robert said. "We'll be right back."

Toni blinked, wondering what was going on. Robert was
in a foul mood, and Toni chalked it up to lack of sleep. She
wasn't feeling exactly cheerful herself.

Twenty minutes later, she'd given Bobby's ankle a thorough exam and X-rayed it with the new machine. "It's
sprained, all right. You need to put ice on it and keep it
elevated for twenty-four hours. If the swelling doesn't start
going down, let me know."

"I'm hungry," Bobby said.

"Hungry?" Robert said. "We just ate an hour ago!"

"I've got some pizza—"

"Yuck. I like bacon and eggs," Bobby said, scowling.

"Takes after you," Toni said, sneaking a wry smile to Robert.

He didn't smile back. "We need to talk," he mouthed.

Toni nodded, wondering what was going on. Robert acted like the stranger he'd been when he brought Mr. Tankersly in. And there was a reserved coldness about him.

"We aren't going to marry you," Bobby blurted.

Toni blinked, squinted her eyes, and tried to make sense of what Bobby said.

"Bob-by!"

Bobby looked up at his father.

"Well, you said—"

"I know what I said. But it isn't your place to—" Robert stopped, scraping his fingers through his springy hair. He shut his eyes and took a deep breath as tense, thick silence wrapped around them like an old blanket.

Toni couldn't breathe, her chest tightening in anguish. *It isn't your place to tell her.* That's what Robert was about to say. Tell her what? That Robert had been forced to choose between her and Bobby? Toni knew that's what happened. She didn't need a microscope to study the situation. It stuck out like an ugly goiter on the side of someone's otherwise smooth neck. Why had she ever let the man kiss her?

"I need to get you to Mrs. Sellers, Bobby," Robert said without looking at Toni. "I'm starting a new job today."

Toni crossed her arms, narrowing her eyes. So this was it? He was going to just waltz out of here like nothing ever happened? *Not on your life, Mister.*

"We need to talk, *now,*" she said through clenched teeth.

"I'll be back," Robert said as he picked up Bobby.

"D-a-d. I thought you said you weren't going to—"

145

Robert clamped his hand over Bobby's mouth. "I'll be back in an hour."

Fifty-nine minutes later, Toni sat in the office with Robert across from her. The smell of stale pizza and strong, black coffee permeated the room. Neither had said a word. Not even hello. Toni waited on Robert to open the conversation.

He swallowed. "This is hard."

"Just tell me what happened. I'm a big girl."

Anxiety crinkling the corners of his eyes, Robert tugged the edge of his mustache. "The reason Bobby hurt his ankle was because he fell out the window. He was running away."

"Running away? Why?"

Robert's expressive eyes answered the unasked question.

"I see," Toni whispered, leaning back in her chair.

"He's more upset about—about us than I thought. I thought—" Robert stood and, shoving his hands in his jeans pocket, looked out the window. "I thought he'd come around. I'd convinced myself that he'd start likin' you if he just got to know you."

"But he can't stand me," Toni said, her throat constricting. She didn't know why she was so upset about this, why her heart thudded in heavy, disappointing beats. Toni had suspected this might happen, and she knew she should have had the sense to end the relationship before it took on hurricane proportions. But that didn't stop the ache.

Robert turned back to face her. "I really don't think it's you, Toni. I think he's just scared. I think it would be the same with anybody."

This would have been much easier if Robert's dark eyes weren't full of regret and something close to sorrow. If he were being rude or arrogant or bossy like he'd been earlier this morning, she could turn to anger to get her through

146

this. But with him looking at her like his heart was breaking as much as hers, Toni had to suppress the threatening tears.

"So it's over. Is that what you're saying?"

Robert remained silent, gazing at her as if the words were alien to even his ears. "I'm afraid so," he finally rasped out. "I promised him I'd . . . I—I just can't do it to him. He's already been through so much. I just can't—"

Toni stood. "I understand." All she wanted now was to be alone. Quiet. Empty. Alone.

"I'm sorry," he whispered, walking toward her. As he touched her cheek, Toni noticed the pools forming in his eyes. "I had no intention of this happening. I didn't want to hurt you. I—you know how I feel about you."

"I know," Toni said, her eyes blurring. She took a deep, shaky breath. "I think it would be good if you left now."

"Toni . . ."

"Just go. . . ." Toni closed her eyes. A hot tear slid down her cheek. "Please."

"All right. If that's what you want."

"It's what I want."

CHAPTER 18

One week later. 7:00 a.m. Toni sat straight up in bed, her chest tight, her heart pounding. Like a cor nered bobcat, she peered around her peach and beige bedroom. Something woke her up. She didn't know what it was, but—

The telephone shrilled. She jumped. Her chest relaxing, Toni inhaled in relief. "Just the phone, Kirkpatrick. It was just the phone," she mumbled to herself, reaching to answer the telephone on her nightstand. This was her day off, and she'd planned to sleep in. So much for that.

"Hello."

"Dr. Kirkpatrick?" a man's urgent voice asked.

Toni heard moaning in the background. "Yes."

"Derek Davidson. I'm at the hotel. There's a young woman here who's—"

A pain-filled cry cut off Derek's words. "Is she okay?" he mumbled to someone else in the room.

Toni rolled out of bed, recognizing the sound of panic in the woman's screams. "What room are you in?" she asked, cramming her feet into the penny loafers next to her bed.

"Two-fifty," Derek said. "You better get here, fast. I think this baby's coming now." The line went dead.

Not taking the time to dress, Toni grabbed her yellow robe, putting it on as she gathered her car keys and doctor's bag. Looked like it was going to be one of those days.

Twenty minutes later, Toni passed a screaming, baby boy to Derek. "Wrap him up in a towel," she ordered, turning back to finish with the mother. She'd arrived just in time to deliver the baby, and barely that. Toni had to ask directions to room two-fifty from the front desk.

The young, Native American father smiled at her with frightened yet relieved eyes.

Someone burst through the doorway. "What's goin' on in here?" a familiar voice asked.

Toni gritted her teeth. Robert. She glanced toward him. "We've just had a baby. Could you help?" She looked at the new mother. "He's a paramedic, don't worry."

The man had a knack for showing up every time she left the house. But what was he doing here? *Stay calm,* she told her racing heart.

With Robert's help, Toni finished with the mother and covered her.

"You did call the hospital?" she asked Derek for the third time.

Derek nodded, handing the baby to his father. "They're on their way." Smoothing a shaking hand over his soggy hair Derek said, "That was a close call." He rested his hands just above the line of his yellow and black swimming trunks.

The young father looked at Toni, anxiety filling his eyes. He didn't appear to be much older than eighteen or nine-

149

teen. "We can't afford to go to the hospital. We don't have enough money."

His companion nodded, her brown eyes wide.

"But you need to make sure everything's okay. They'll run some tests on the baby, and take care of you until you can get back on your feet. It'll only be a day or two." Toni suspected the two weren't married and had run away together to have the baby. There was probably a set or two of disapproving parents involved. She'd seen it all too often.

Toni felt Robert's gaze on her. She glanced up to see the kind of admiration in his eyes only one professional can have for another. He'd been loads of help at first. But now that they'd done all they could, he was really making her nervous.

"But we don't have enough money," the young man said again as if Toni hadn't heard him the first time.

"They have funds for—"

"I'll take care of it," Derek said, compassion filling his light green eyes. Toying with the towel hanging from his neck, Derek leaned over the squirming baby and touched his damp cheek. "I kinda like this little guy."

Toni's eyes widened for a split second. She'd just taken a long enough look at Derek to realize what he was wearing—swimming trunks, and a towel around his neck. And his hair was wet as if he'd been in the water.

Toni's gaze darted to Robert's. A silent communication flashed between them. Robert already knew. Toni guessed he'd known when he came pushing in here.

The young man laid the baby by its mother and the two became lost in their own world.

"How'd you discover them, Derek?" Toni mumbled, thinking of what Robert said about the criminal hanging himself.

"I was taking a quick swim. This room's right over the

pool. I heard her screaming," he whispered and then shrugged. "You know the rest." Derek seemed too shaken from his close encounter with delivering a baby to realize he'd just as good as told them he'd lied about why he didn't rescue Mr. Tankersly.

But could this man, who's eyes were full of concern for complete strangers, be a murderer?

"Could I talk to you for a few minutes?" Robert asked.

Toni shook her head, glancing at the baby before following Robert into the hall. She didn't really want to be alone with him, not even in a hotel walkway.

"I'm going to talk to Sheriff Braxton," Robert whispered. "He needs to haul Derek in for questioning."

Trying to avoid eye contact, Toni stared at the top button of Robert's navy shirt and nodded. Inhaling the smell of chlorine, she wondered why Robert brought her out here anyway. He didn't have to clear his actions with her. And standing only two feet from him made her empty stomach churn.

"I've been watching him. I knew I could catch him at something that would get him in trouble sooner or later. I snuck into the hotel and hid over there after I saw him headin' for the pool this mornin'." Robert pointed across the large, indoor swimming pool to the dressing area. "And just like I figured, he jumped in and started swimmin' like a dolphin. I snuck back out and was two blocks away, headin' toward the sheriff's office when I saw you drive by."

Robert hesitated and gave his moustache a tug. "I, I was afraid you might be goin' into a bad situation in here, what with all that's happened. That's why I came. I, I started not to, but decided it couldn't hurt."

Toni nodded. "Thanks for covering my tracks," she mumbled, looking toward the pool's sparkling water, looking anywhere other than in his eyes. "Do you really think Derek tried to kill Mr. Tankersly? He just seems so nice."

151

"I noticed," Robert said. "I don't know. But I do know he's lied to us—twice. And he'd better have a humdinger of a reason for doing it. Otherwise . . ."

"Well, I need to get back to my patient." She turned to go back into the room, ready to get away from Robert.

"Wait," he said, grabbing her arm. "How, how have you been?"

Toni swallowed, looking into his eyes before she could stop herself. Yes. The pain, the misery, the concern were all still there just as they'd been every time Toni had seen him in the last week. And that seemed to be almost every day. He'd turned up in the grocery store, at church, in the diner. . . . The list went on and on.

"Fine," she heard herself saying. "Fine" was such a non-committal answer. But what else could she say? That the last week had been the most lonely week of her life? Her mom always told her you didn't know what you'd missed as long as you didn't have it. Well, Toni knew what had been missing in her life now. And it was more than Sylvester and that impostor bird could give her.

"How's Bobby?" she asked, stepping away from his touch.

Robert nodded. "Fine."

"Okay, well, I guess I'll see you 'round."

"Yeah," he said, working his jaw muscles.

Gripping the steering wheel until her hands ached, Toni drove the short distance to her home. Why did she have to fall for the most ineligible bachelor in Colorado? She'd figured the longer she stayed away from him, the less it would hurt to see him. But Toni honestly thought it was getting worse. And short of moving, there wasn't anything she could do about it. But she could do something to control her wayward thoughts.

Trying to force Robert's warm gaze out of her mind, she

turned her thoughts to what would happen with Derek. Toni's latest clues about Sylvia's over-interest in the burglary hadn't given Sheriff Braxton much to go on. After all, a lot of people owned a blue sweater, including her. And most neighbors were a little nosy. But Toni knew this discovery about Derek was something completely different. He could have saved Mr. Tankersly, and he didn't. Sheriff Braxton would definitely question him about it.

But there was something else bothering Toni about this thing with Derek. She wasn't really sure what it was. Toni felt as if she'd seen something or maybe Derek had said something that would incriminate him even more, or perhaps completely exonerate him. But she just couldn't put her finger on it.

Toni slowed as she neared the turn to her street. Then accelerating, she steered toward home. But she noticed someone pulling out of her driveway in a hurry. Toni squinted to determine who it was. The green sedan wasn't familiar to her. But as Toni drew closer, she recognized the driver. Barbara Jones occupied the front seat. Toni waved. She and Barbara had become friends during the few times Toni had checked on Mr. Tankersly. Not looking in Toni's direction, Barbara sped past her.

Puzzled, Toni parked, got out of her car, and went through her front door. But something awaited her which completely removed all thoughts of Barbara, Derek, and Robert from her mind.

CHAPTER 19

"Derek can swim," Robert said, sitting down across from the sheriff.

Sheriff Braxton's eyes widened. "How'd you find out?"

"I've been watching him. I saw him walkin' toward the part of the hotel that has the pool in it this morning around seven. So I hid where I could see him. Sure enough, he was strokin' through that water like a pro." Robert didn't mention he'd also seen Toni Kirkpatrick. He didn't want to think about her. But how could a man get the picture of sleepy gray eyes, tousled reddish-blond hair, and peachy lips out of his mind?

"Good job, son. We need to get him cornered now and give him the 'what for.' "

"Give 'em enough rope and they usually hang themselves," Robert muttered. "But not always," he added, thinking about how sly Wayne Freeman had been. Could he forgive someone who'd betrayed him so? Toni seemed to think he could. Robert knew he'd need more power than he had within himself to do it. But he just wasn't ready.

"I wonder if 'murder number one' fits Derek, though," Sheriff Braxton said, standing. "And I want to know what kind of motive he has."

Robert stood. "Let me know what you find out. I've gotta get to work."

"Oh no you don't," Sheriff Braxton said, putting a hand on Robert's arm. "I want to know when you're going to say yes to my job offer."

Robert shook his head. "I already told you—"

"Sheriff Braxton," Alice said from the office door. "There's a young woman here to see you."

"I'll get out of here so you can do your job," Robert said, walking toward the door.

"Send her in," Sheriff Braxton said, pointing at Robert. "And you're not off the hook yet."

Smiling, Robert tilted his straw cowboy hat. He was strongly tempted to tell the sheriff yes. He had to face it, his handyman business might be a success, but he was bored bootless. Yet Robert just didn't know if he were ready to face those memories. "See ya 'round," he said, putting the sheriff off once more. He turned to leave and halted, his heart skidding to a stop.

Toni stood just inside the office. She'd changed into a cream-colored sweat suit since he saw her. And even though she still didn't have on a speck of makeup, she'd brushed her hair into shining silkiness and sprayed that confounded perfume on. Why'd she have to go and do that?

"Hey, Doc!" Sheriff Braxton said. "What can I do for you?"

Toni glanced at Robert. He hadn't moved since he'd seen her, and Robert knew she was wondering whether or not he was going to keep walking toward the door. Well, he'd just had a sudden change in plans.

"I—" She turned her gaze to Sheriff Braxton. "I came to tell you my jewelry turned up." Toni slowly raised the yellow pillowcase she carried as if she didn't quite believe the words she'd just spoken.

"What?" Robert and the sheriff asked together.

"My jewelry. It—"

"Where'd you find it?" Robert asked, his eyes wide with surprise.

"It was just inside my door when I came home after delivering the baby. Sylvester was batting around this pillowcase. I knew it wasn't mine because all my sheet sets are peach. So I picked it up and there was the jewelry!"

Toni nervously chewed her bottom lip.

"How do you think it got there? I mean, was there any sign of someone breaking in?" Sheriff Braxton asked.

Toni shrugged. "No. The only thing I can figure is somebody must've put it through my mail slot."

"Is it all there?" Robert asked, nodding toward the pillowcase. He crossed his arms, wishing he could ignore what the morning sun filtering through the window was doing to the red highlights in Toni's hair.

"No. There's an emerald ring missing and its matching pendant and earrings." She looked at Robert. "The earrings I had on at your—" She stopped, pressing her lips together.

At my place—the first night I kissed you. The night the universe stood still, Robert thought. He looked at his teak-colored ostrich boots, heavy tension creating a knot in his chest, in his stomach, in his heart. Why did life have to be so complicated?

Sheriff Braxton cleared his throat, giving Robert a curious glance. Apparently the grapevine was behind on this one. "Can you tell me everything that happened from the time you left until you found the jewelry? Somethin' might click. Here, take a seat." He motioned toward the chairs across from his desk. "You too, boy."

156

Toni and Robert sat down. She wouldn't look at him, and he couldn't say he blamed her.

"Okay. Derek Davidson called about a girl having a baby at his hotel. So I went and delivered the baby. Then after the helicopter ambulance picked her up, I drove back home. And on the way home, I saw . . . Barbara Jones . . . pulling out of my driveway." Toni stared at the sheriff as if a thought had slowly dawned on her.

"Frank's wife?" the sheriff asked.

"Yes."

"We may have something," Braxton said.

"And I waved. But she didn't see me—or didn't look at me. I thought she didn't see me, but—"

"But she may have ignored you on purpose," Robert said, tempted to tell the sheriff to hand him a deputy badge so he could jump into this with all fours like he'd wanted to from the first.

"Right," Sheriff Braxton said.

"But if Barbara brought back my jewelry, how did she get it in the first place?" Toni asked.

"There's only one way to find out," Robert said, giving in to the temptation. "I'm going to need a deputy badge, Sheriff. But I want you to know this is only part-time and it's only until this case is solved. And I'm not running for sheriff."

"Whatever you say, son," Sheriff Braxton said, smiling like Sam's big bullfrog. He fumbled through his desk drawer and handed Robert a silver badge. "We'll get your uniforms ordered as soon as possible."

"I'll go question Barbara while you question Derek—"

"No," Toni said, standing.

"No, what?" Robert asked, noticing the inflexible gleam he'd seen in her gray eyes more than once.

"No. I don't want you going out there and asking Barbara a bunch of questions. What if she didn't put the jewelry in my house? What if she was only coming for a visit—maybe to tell me something about her father. She'll think I think she's in on this somehow."

"She might be," Robert said.

Toni scrutinized him. "Barbara Jones is one of the most gentle women I've ever met. She couldn't be involved in theft and murder."

"You said yourself she was pulling out of your driveway when you drove up. And you're the one who connected her with the jewelry. Now you're trying to tell me you don't think she's in on it?"

"That's exactly what I'm saying."

"Well I do. And I'm going to find out for myself." Robert crossed his arms, daring her to defy him.

Toni stepped toward him, placing her index finger in the middle of his chest. "You'll do no such thing, Robert Hooper. That woman's been through enough already." She removed her finger. "Somebody tried to kill her father, and she doesn't know who it is. Mr. Tankersly's finally starting to show some improvement. But Frank hates him and doesn't even want her to go see him. And if she's not on the verge of a nervous breakdown, I'll eat my stethoscope. I don't want you going out there, asking a bunch of questions, and, and making rude insinuations. I didn't come here to cause trouble for Barbara. I—"

"Rude insinuations? I've never made rude insinuations in my life. I need to find out what's goin' on here, and I'm gonna do it." Placing his hands on his hips, Robert fought the urge to grab this stubborn woman and kiss her—kiss her right here in front of Sheriff Braxton and Alice, and anybody else who cared to watch. She was the most obstinate woman he'd ever—

"Well, there are a lot of things that go on, as you put it, Mr. Hooper, that aren't resolved," she said evenly. "But I don't think Barbara's the one this time."

158

Sheriff Braxton cleared his throat.

Robert ignored him, his nerves screaming with what she'd just said. Her words were loaded with accusations which circled him like angry hornets. Robert knew he'd hurt her, but it had hurt him too.

"That wasn't fair," he said, his voice thick.

"Neither is life," she said tightly, turning to walk out of the office.

"Toni." Robert followed her, not knowing why. He just didn't want her leaving like this. "Toni!"

She answered his call with a slammed door.

Robert walked back into the office, his heart thudding with irritation and confusion. He was beginning to wonder if he should think about moving. He didn't want to uproot Bobby again. But at the same time, he didn't know if he could stand living in the same town with her much longer. What if she got married? It'd kill him.

"Well, now doesn't that beat all?" Sheriff Braxton asked as he walked toward the door. "These women, I'll tell you . . ." He slapped Robert's shoulder. "But don't you go worrying about it now, son. I've seen this kinda thing before. I don't know what's got you and her actin' like two negative ends of a magnet, but I'm willing to stake my new set of steel-belted radials that it'll all work out."

"Yeah," Robert said, knowing the sheriff was wrong. Even a miracle wouldn't remove Bobby's scars and dissolve his fears. They'd have to go back in time and change the past. And that just wouldn't happen.

"Well, I've got to make a trip to the Jones's place, and you've got to talk to Derek," Robert said, heading out the door.

CHAPTER 20

The next evening. 9:30 p.m.

Toweling her hair dry, Toni wished she could rub all thoughts of Robert Hooper from her mind. She stepped into her bedroom and reached to flip on the light. Her hand stopped.

Something was wrong.

She felt as if someone were in the house with her. Toni's heart pounded, the hair on her arms prickling. Whirling around, she peered up the dark hall.

Nobody. Rubbing her arms, Toni bit her lip. She felt it. Somebody was watching her. Toni didn't know what to do. Should she tear down the hall or run into her bedroom and slam the door? The skin along her backbone turned to gooseflesh.

160

A shadow moved against the far wall.

Toni panted. Someone was in her room.

Turning, she stumbled up the hall, her stomach churning in terrorized nausea.

Heavy footsteps echoed from the bedroom and entered the hall, close behind her. Leaning forward, Toni stretched for the hall's end. If she could just get outside. . . .

Her heart thudded in her ears, mingling with the footsteps closing in on her. Panicking, she tried to scream, but nothing came out.

The footsteps grew closer—only inches away. The intruder's gasps filled the hall, echoing like the sound of death.

Toni's lungs ached as she struggled forward, into the living room, the intruder so close she felt his body heat. She threw herself at the front door, fighting the new lock with hands shaking to dysfunction.

The hard end of a gun ate through her bathrobe and into her ribs. "Oh no you don't," a deep, familiar voice growled.

Toni pressed her trembling body against the door. *Not again*. The gun felt as if it pushed straight through her lung, and she smothered a sob.

He lowered his mouth to her ear. "Where's the jewelry?" His hot, foul breath scorched her skin.

Toni gulped, twisting her head away from the smell.

"Where is it?" he demanded.

"I . . . I don't have it." She inhaled. "Lord—"

"I already told you once, praying won't help you. If you don't cooperate, you'll be dead. Now where's the jewelry?"

Toni didn't think her legs would hold her up much longer. "I—I don't have it," she said again, her voice trembling.

"Don't lie to me." He jiggled the blunt ended gun deeper into her ribs.

Toni flinched in pain as the room tilted.

161

"I know you got it back yesterday. And if you don't fork it over, you won't ever do anything else."

"It isn't here. I put it in a safe." A sob tore through her.

"You're lying." He cocked the gun.

Toni squeezed her eyes shut and panted for air, knowing each breath could be her last. *Help me, Lord!* "I'm not lying," she said in a voice which sounded much calmer than she felt. "Do you think I would lie with a gun on me?"

Her words silenced him, all but his labored breathing. The gun's pressure decreased. "If you're lying to me, I'll find out. I'm closer than you think, pretty lady. I need that jewelry—need the money. Understand?"

Toni nodded. "I understand," she whispered, clutching the door.

He pushed the gun into her back again. "I want you to get it tomorrow, and I'll be by to pick it up. Understand?"

"When?"

"You leave that up to me. Just be ready. And don't do anything stupid or you'll be murder number three."

A pair of headlights pierced the darkness, flooding Toni's driveway, illuminating the living room. A truck's familiar rumble filled the house.

A warm rush of blood flooded Toni's face. *Robert.*

With a curse, the man pulled the gun away from her ribs and ran toward Toni's bedroom.

Biting her bottom lip, Toni fought the panic urging her to hysteria. She attacked the lock and threw open the door. Wild instinct demanded she escape the house.

Tripping across the porch, Toni flew down the steps and ran into a hard, masculine body. A pair of arms steadied her.

"Whoa there."

"Robert." Throwing herself against him, Toni clung to his warm, safe strength, not caring that the last words they'd exchanged weren't exactly friendly or that she didn't have a right to hold him close.

"What a welcome!" he said in surprise.

Toni pushed against him. "There was a man in my house," she whispered urgently, "just now when you drove up."

Robert dropped his arms and pulled a gun from a holster. Hurrying up the steps, he flung the door open.

Left standing in the darkness, Toni felt as if someone lurked behind every tree. Her skin prickled. She didn't want to go back inside until she knew it was safe, but the house beat the feeling the shadows gave her.

Scurrying up the steps, she whipped through the door, slammed it, locked it, and leaned against it for support. Robert's boots thudded through the back of the house. Holding her breath, Toni hoped the man hadn't escaped. But at the same time, she hoped he had. Toni didn't want Robert to get hurt.

His footsteps echoed from the hall, and he went outside. In a matter of minutes, Robert rushed into the living room, replacing the gun in its holster. His jeans and faded denim shirt looked as tired as he did.

"Are you okay?" he asked, wrapping his arms around her before Toni knew his intention.

She nodded, her pulse quickening at the protective fire burning in his eyes.

Just as fast as he'd drawn her into his arms, Robert planted a kiss on her lips that reflected the time they had spent away from each other.

Toni's first reaction was to respond, loving his nearness, his warmth . . . him. Her breath quickened with the pressure of Robert's fingers spreading across her back. He pulled her closer, pressing the place where the gun had been embedded in her ribcage. An arrow of pain shot up Toni's spine, quickly landing her in reality.

Wrenching her lips from his, she pushed away. "What

are you doing?" she asked incredulously, backing up. Her mind was full of leftover fear and new fury. How dare he come in here and—

"I was kissing you. Or have you forgotten what that feels like?" he asked tilting his chin sarcastically.

"You arrogant . . . you don't have the right to come in here and kiss me like that. It isn't fair!"

"Well, neither is life," he said quietly, the sarcastic tilt gone from his chin.

Toni breathed in heavy, deliberate spurts as silence invaded the living room just as the man had invaded her bedroom only minutes before. Robert had used her own line on her. And she deserved it. Toni knew she hadn't acted fairly yesterday, but she'd been too shaken to think straight.

"I—I'm sorry I said what I did yesterday," she said to her fireplace.

"I'm sorry, too," Robert said, his words taking on a bigger meaning than just this situation. "I shouldn't have kissed you. You're right. But just because we're—just because I can't see you any more doesn't mean my feelings have changed. And I was glad to see you alive. That's all."

Toni dared to look at him. He stood with his hands on his hips, a dark shadow stirring his inky eyes.

"He broke out your bedroom window," Robert said. "The reason I stopped by was to tell you the locks I ordered came in. I was going to install them tomorrow, but it doesn't look like locks are going to make any difference. You need some steel bars."

Toni shivered.

"Your jewelry box is all messed up again, and there's no jewelry, either."

"I put it in the safe at the clinic."

"Good," Robert said, relief filling his voice.

Wrapping her arms around her, Toni trembled as her

164

throat tightened. She didn't know if her nerves could take much more, if her *heart* could take much more. Running had grown appealing.

She inhaled and winced as another sharp pain shot from her ribcage.

"Toni?"

She swallowed against the dry feeling invading her mouth as acid burned her throat. "I—I think I need some water." Toni sank to the couch.

Robert rushed to the kitchen, returning with a glass of water.

She gulped it, the coolness washing away her mouth's dryness and calming her throat's burning.

"Tell me what happened," he said after a few minutes. He sat on the couch at a safe distance, his eyes still full of the protective fire she'd seen before he kissed her.

Toni took a deep breath and told Robert everything. " . . . and he said he was coming back for the jewelry tomorrow, and if I didn't cooperate I'd be murder number three."

"Murder number three?" Robert stood, pacing the living room.

Toni watched him walk from the fireplace, to the couch, and back, like a restless bull. Her house was so full with him, so empty without him—just like her heart.

Toni blinked as the intruder's words sank into her thoughts. Murder number one. Murder number three.

"Who was number two?" Robert asked

"Do you think Sheriff Braxton might have been right when he said Mr. Tankersly knew he was number one in a series of murders?"

"Maybe, but who's number two?" Robert sat in the chair by the fireplace and stared at Toni as if she weren't there.

"I don't know," Toni said. Then something clicked in her mind. "I don't think that's what it is," she rushed, vividly remembering what had teased her thoughts when she delivered that baby. There'd been something to do with Derek, and now she knew what it was. She licked her lips. "When Derek called yesterday morning, I had to go to the lobby to get instructions on where room two-fifty was. The street address was on the outside of the hotel's entrance. . . ." Toni stopped, stunned. She still couldn't believe someone as nice as Derek . . . but the evidence said otherwise.

"And?" Robert said, leaning forward.

"And it said Number One. The hotel's on Sixth Avenue. So the address is Number One Sixth Avenue."

"Murder number one," Robert said, standing.

"That's it," Toni said.

"Or is it? I mean, did the man who broke in here seem like Derek to you?"

"I—I don't know." Toni shut her eyes, trying to recall anything incriminating. "He was about my height like Derek, but so is Uncle Phil and a lot of other men."

"What about his voice?"

"I know he disguised it. Nobody growls like that." A former thought flashed through Toni's mind. "Derek just seems so nice. It's hard for me to believe . . ."

"I know," Robert said, "but that doesn't really mean anything. I've run across more than one criminal who didn't look or act the part." His lips twisted in bitterness as silence settled between them.

Someone knocked, and Toni jumped.

Robert stood, approaching the door like a lion scouting out a gazelle. He peered out the small window, then opened the door.

"Hello," Sylvia Cornelius said. "I—I saw your truck over here, and—and was wondering if you'd found Derek yet?" Her voice sounded as shrill as high C on an organ.

Toni peered toward the door. Sylvia wrung her hands in worry, and her jeans and red sweatshirt looked as if she'd slept in them. Had Derek pulled a disappearing act? Had he

166

realized he'd incriminated himself past exoneration?

"We still haven't located him," Robert answered. "I assume he hasn't called?"

"No," Sylvia said. "I—I left Jeff by himself. I need to get back home." And she was gone.

"Has Derek disappeared?" Toni asked.

"Yeah. Sheriff Braxton went to question him yesterday after you left, and he couldn't find him—anywhere. None of the hotel employees have a clue where he went. His Mercedes is gone."

"Do you think he realized he'd given himself away and ran?"

Robert started pacing the room again. "That's what we were thinking. But if the same man who broke in here tonight is the one who stole your jewelry in the first place, could it be Derek if he's not even in Ouray?"

"Good point. If he's out of town, how could he have broken into my house?"

"Right. And just supposing Mr. Tankersly was talking about Derek when he said, 'Murder Number One,' we still don't know how 'Murder Number Three' fits in. I mean, Sheriff Braxton could have been right on the series murder speculation."

"And Derek's address could just be a coincidence." Toni thought a minute. "But his leaving town looks very suspicious."

"Wait a minute, we don't really know for sure that he is out of town. Nobody actually saw him leave," Robert said. "Besides, I think Sylvia knows something she isn't telling. I questioned her yesterday. She was as nervous as a stallion near a rattlesnake, but she wouldn't admit she knew a thing."

"What about Barbara?" Toni figured Robert had gone to question her in spite of Toni's objections. "Did she say she knew anything about how my jewelry showed back up?"

Robert shook his head. "She seemed a little nervous, but she said she'd just come for a visit. Said she didn't notice you when you waved."

"She's really had a hard time of it," Toni said. "I hope your questions didn't upset her too much."

Robert raised his brows. "Just for the record, I didn't make rude insinuations."

Toni stared at him, not able to come up with one word in reply. She was tired of having to carry on a conversation with the man who'd broken her heart. They were both more than a little testy, and Toni was ready to get away from him.

She was ready to get away from this house too. Toni didn't want to stay here tonight or any night until this was solved. She was through with being brave and not running. And she was almost through with holding back the resentment which threatened to engulf her. This man—whoever he was—was ruining her life. She was tired of it all! Emotionally and spiritually she was nearing exhaustion.

"You aren't staying here any longer," Robert said. "I don't care if I have to tie you up and haul you over to your uncle and aunt's myself."

Toni gritted her teeth. "I've already decided that."

"And I will be there tomorrow mornin' to escort you to work and watch you all day."

"If you insist," Toni said, half relieved somebody would be there in case that lunatic tried to attack her. Yet the other half of her was annoyed with Robert's bossiness. "But I'm not some two year old who needs to be ordered around."

"No, but you're about as stubborn as one."

Toni opened her mouth, ready to tell him he should know because he was an expert on the subject himself, when he smiled.

"And I don't think I'd want you any other way."

Toni caught her breath as neither spoke. "Robert . . ." She shut her eyes, trying to block out the boyish charm which had a way of twisting her heart into knots. She couldn't continue seeing him everywhere she went, knowing there was a barrier neither of them could cross. "Something's going to have to give. I . . . I cannot keep this up. Either I'm going to have to move, or—"

"Or I will," he said.

"You can't. What about Bobby?" She opened her eyes.

Robert turned away from her in frustration. "I know. I've thought of that. He's settled in here. Made friends. He's spendin' the night with Sam again tonight. Sam was at my house last night. I'd hate to uproot him, but it might be better than—"

"I'll go," Toni said. "Dad and Mom'll be glad. I guess moving here was just a pipe dream, anyway." She swallowed.

"But that isn't fair to you. I'll—"

"Life—isn't fair."

CHAPTER 21

The next morning, Toni stared into the bird cage. Her impostor bird had slowly grown accustomed to his new surroundings, and he welcomed her home with merry chirping. Toni was considering naming him. It didn't look like she'd ever see Tweety Bird again.

"I think he likes you," Uncle Phil said from the couch.

Toni replaced the bird's water and pulled out his seed. "Yeah. But I wish I knew about Tweety Bird." She swallowed. "I wonder if he's alive, even. Or if that man—"

"I'm sure he's probably okay," Uncle Phil said, standing. "Why don't you go put on your work clothes, and I'll feed Sylvester for you."

Hearing his name, Sylvester meowed from the kitchen.

"He should've been a pig," Toni muttered. "I fed him last night before I left."

Uncle Phil had refused to let Toni come home by herself to dress for work and feed her pets, and she was glad. Toni

170

had had as many close calls as she wanted.

Robert and Sheriff Braxton had dusted for prints last night and boarded up her broken window. Toni dreaded going back to that room.

Having replenished the bird's seed, she turned toward her bedroom to change for work. A knock at the door stopped her.

"I'll get it," Uncle Phil said.

"No. I will. I'm closer." Approaching the door, she gazed out the front window, searching for a vehicle in her driveway. But there wasn't one. She peered out the door's window cautiously. Toni was on edge even in broad daylight.

But the two people staring up at her weren't ones to get on edge about. Smiling, Toni opened the door, wondering why Bobby Hooper and Sam Martin would be paying her a visit.

"Hi, boys," Toni said, her heart aching with how much Bobby resembled Robert. Could it be possible that somehow Bobby had undergone a change of heart?

"Hello," Bobby and Sam uttered together.

"Would you like to come in?" Toni asked curiously, wondering to what she owed this visit.

Bobby nodded, picking up a bird cage sitting slightly behind him which Toni hadn't noticed before. A green-blue parakeet jumped to the side of the cage, and Toni's heart quickened with pleasure.

"You found Tweety Bird?" she asked as the two walked into her living room.

Bobby set the cage on a nearby table. "Well . . . um—"

"I can't believe it!" Toni said, beaming. "You guys are too much! Where'd you find him?" She peered at the bird, anxious to let her feathered friend out of his cage so he could restake his territory. If she didn't know any better, she'd say Tweety Bird was smiling. He jumped to the other side of the cage and whistled loudly.

171

"We . . . um . . ." Sam said, his hazel eyes apprehensive as he looked past Toni and into the kitchen. Bobby gazed in that direction also.

Toni looked over her shoulder at Uncle Phil.

"I think I'll go sit out on the porch for a few minutes," he said, excusing himself.

"We didn't find him," Bobby blurted as soon as the front door shut.

"What?" Toni said, her mind reeling in confusion. "Well if you didn't find him . . . how did you . . ." she trailed off, the significance of this visit hitting her like a slap in the face with a two-by-four.

Her expression must have said exactly what she thought because Sam said, "You won't tell our parents, will you?" He brushed his straight, blond bangs out of his eyes in a nervous gesture.

"Please don't tell Dad," Bobby added. "He'll kill me."

Toni's face grew cold. "You two stole my bird?"

They nodded and studied their sneakers. "We left you my bird," Sam said. "Her name's Blue Girl."

"Why?" Toni asked, her eyes wide with hurt and confusion.

Bobby cleared his throat. "I thought, well . . . I thought that if . . . if you got . . . got scared enough you might . . . might move, because I didn't . . . didn't like you."

"So we decided to get your bird and teach him how to say 'I hate you,' " Sam rushed.

Toni flinched. "Do you really hate me, Bobby?"

"I don't know." He shrugged. "But we were gonna bring him back! We kept the key and after we . . . we taught him to say . . . to say. . . that . . . we were gonna bring him back. Honest!" Pausing, he stared at the floor. "But Dad changed the locks."

Toni could hardly believe what she was hearing. "How'd you know where the key was?"

172

"I was here when Dad fixed your window." He pointed toward the window next to the fireplace.

"He saw where you kept your key," Sam said.

"And you also saw that white toy car with the snake, didn't you?"

"Yes." Shoving his hands in his jeans pocket, Bobby continued to stare downward.

"And so you just waltzed right in here, took my bird, and left the car and Sam's bird?" Toni asked, an edge to her voice, a lump of ice in her heart. "Do you know what you two have put me through? Do you know how worried I was that somebody was in my house, somebody who might try to kill me? And Bobby Hooper, you just . . . just sat out there in that truck the whole time your Dad changed my locks and didn't say a word!" Toni had never wanted to turn a child over her knee more than now.

Bobby swallowed. "I . . . I know it was bad. That's . . . that's why we brought him back."

"Yeah," Sam said. "We got ta feelin' bad."

"And we were afraid if Sam's mom found out, she'd . . . she'd kill us."

"How'd you keep it from her this long?"

"Sam's bird lives in his room."

"Yeah. But my bird don't talk and—"

"And he was afraid Tweety Bird would say somethin', and his mom would find out." Bobby turned a pleading, dark gaze on Toni. "Please don't tell on us, Dr. Kirkpatrick."

"Please," Sam begged.

"We didn't teach him to say 'I hate you,' " Bobby added. "We chickened out."

Toni chewed her bottom lip, some of her anger receding. If she told Robert and the Martins, Toni didn't doubt that the boys might think they were going to die before their parents got through with them. If she ever had a child who

173

did something like this Toni would probably ground him for life.

She sighed and had to admit it took a lot of guts to bring Tweety Bird back. And more than likely, the two had put themselves under as much, if not more, misery than their parents could.

"I won't tell them," she said, hoping she was doing the right thing.

"You won't?" Bobby asked, astonishment lighting his eyes.

"You mean you really won't?" Sam added.

"I mean I really won't," Toni said, wondering how she was going to tell Sheriff Braxton and Robert that Tweety Bird was back home without telling them how he got there.

CHAPTER 22

Toni stared unseeing at Mr. Zimmerman's file. Having Robert Hooper lurking around every corner in the clinic had Toni's nerves in a tight wad right in the pit of her stomach. But he'd kept his word about watching her all day. Toni wondered when—or if—the killer would strike. She also wondered when—or if—she were going to have the guts to tell Robert the killer hadn't taken Tweety Bird.

She hadn't even mentioned anything about moving back to Little Rock to her uncle and aunt yet, either. Toni knew their reaction wouldn't be good. They never had any children, and Toni was the closest thing to a daughter for them. They enjoyed having her in the same town.

Robert entered the office and sat down across from her. "Marge just got off the phone with Barbara. She says Mr. Tankersly's starting to squeeze their hands when they ask him to. Things are soundin' good."

"Great. Maybe he'll be able to talk soon." *And this will be over,* Toni added to herself. She rubbed her eyes. She'd had a long day, and even though it was only three, she had a splitting headache. With no more patients coming, Toni wanted to get away from the clinic and take in some fresh air.

"I think I'm going for a run," she said.

Flicking his wrist, Robert checked his watch. "Heather Martin's going to drop Bobby off here in about five minutes. When he gets here, I'll take you to change. And we'll go together. You can run right outside of town, and Bobby and I will keep an eye on you."

"No," Toni blurted. She didn't want to spend the afternoon with a little boy who didn't like her and a man who couldn't like her.

Robert's brows rose. "We don't bite."

"I know that," she snapped. "But I thought you said you promised Bobby—"

"I've already talked to Bobby. I told him I was acting as your watchdog right now, and . . ." he shrugged, ". . . that's just the way it is."

"Well, it's nothing person—" Toni broke off her words. Yes, it was something very personal. She cleared her throat. "I'll see if Uncle Phil can go with me. I just need some space. I'm feeling stifled."

"Your uncle's having trouble with his back, if you remember correctly."

Toni blinked. Uncle Phil had gone home shortly after lunch to put ice on his back. "I forgot."

"So it's me, or you don't go."

"What about Sheriff Braxton?"

Robert shook his head. "No go. He's out beating the bushes for Derek."

Toni wanted to scream with frustration. "Okay, I'll let you take me."

"But you'd rather be boiled in oil?"

Gritting her teeth, she checked her watch and tried to ignore his sarcasm. He had to know this was just as hard on her as it was on him.

Three minutes had elapsed since Robert said Bobby would be here in five. She had to tell Robert that Tweety Bird was back home today, and Toni knew she shouldn't do it in front of Bobby. *Here goes.*

"I . . . there's something I've got to tell you," she said, looking at the shiny badge attached to the left shoulder of his red plaid shirt.

"Okay, shoot."

Toni pulled on the neck of her yellow blouse and darted a glance at his face. Robert had looked strained ever since the clinic opened, and she wondered if it were her presence or the dark possibilities hanging over this day. After his "boiled in oil" comment, a rebellious side of her hoped she'd added some to his discomfort.

Toni bit her bottom lip and took a deep breath. The spot where the gun's end had wedged into her back sent a sharp pain up her spine. Wincing, she shifted her position.

"You all right?" Robert asked.

"Yeah. It's just that spot where the gun was in my back." She grimaced. "I . . . um . . ." Toni hesitated, knowing Robert was going to bombard her with questions once she told him about her bird. "Tweety Bird's back home," she finally blurted out.

"What?" Robert leaned forward, placing his hands on the desk, his mouth open in surprise. "Did he just appear like he disappeared? Was your house broken into?"

"The answer's 'no' to both of those questions," Toni said, standing.

"Well how'd he get back home, then?" Robert stared up at her and waited for an answer.

Swallowing, Toni opened the bottom desk drawer to

177

remove her purse. "I can't tell you." She made a slow job of shutting the drawer.

"Why?"

"Just trust me on this one."

"But . . . but you might know something here that would incriminate who did it. Maybe solve the case." He stood. "You've got to tell me who—" Robert stopped, a frightened horror filling his eyes. "He didn't . . . didn't blackmail you or threaten you did he?"

Toni smiled slightly, remembering how scared Bobby and Sam had been. "No."

"Toni! Have you lost your mind? Tell me how—"

"I can't," she said. "I'm under oath. And that's final. It's not what you think."

"So Tweety Bird's disappearance doesn't have anything to do with the rest of what's happened to you? Is that what you're saying?"

Toni set her black, leather purse on the desk and removed her lab coat. "Yes." She couldn't say any more. Robert's mind was too sharp. And if he figured out what Bobby did, Bobby would think Toni had told Robert the whole story.

Robert rammed his fingers through his hair. "And you aren't going to tell me any more?"

"No. I wouldn't have told you that much, but I knew you and Sheriff Braxton needed a clear cut picture of all that's happened. And the bird thing wasn't part of it."

He narrowed his eyes.

"Dad?" Bobby called from the front.

"I'm ready if you are," Toni said, walking toward the hall-way.

"Right," Robert said, a speculative gleam in his eyes.

"Give me a second to tell Aunt Marge what I'm up to. She's organizing the back office."

"Right," Robert said again, never taking his gaze off her.

Toni told her aunt where she was going and went back

178

to the waiting room to find Bobby there alone.

"Where's your Dad?" she asked.

"He had to . . . he's in the restroom."

"Oh." She glanced around the mint green walls in discomfort, not knowing what to say.

"Did you tell him?" Bobby asked, his face a mask of worry.

Toni tucked a strand of hair behind her ear and slowly shook her head. Hadn't Bobby believed her when she gave him her word? "I told you I wouldn't tell him, Bobby. And I won't."

His dark eyes calmed somewhat.

"I had to tell him Tweety Bird is back home because he's trying to find out who's been trying to scare me, but I wouldn't tell him how he came home."

"Did he try to make you?"

Toni knelt beside Bobby and chuckled. Bobby knew his father well. "You *bet* he did. But I didn't give an inch."

Bobby took a deep breath. "Thanks. He'd kill me if—"

"Y'all ready to—"

Toni looked over her shoulder to see Robert stopped at the edge of the waiting room, a surprised glimmer in his eyes.

She stood, casting Bobby an uneasy glance. "All ready," she said brightly, trying not to meet Robert's gaze.

"I am," he said in a curious voice.

She and Bobby filed out to Robert's red pickup without a word to Robert or each other. As Robert unlocked his side of the truck, crawled in, and deactivated the electric locks, Toni gave Bobby an exaggerated wink and a thumb's up sign.

For the first time, Bobby smiled at Toni. Toni's heart sang with hope. Maybe she and Bobby could be friends.

"Why do I feel like you two are conspiring against me?" Robert asked as he cranked the truck, astonishment tilting his lips.

179

"Maybe we are," Toni quipped.

"No we aren't," Bobby said, disgust in his voice, a new frown on his face.

Toni's heart sank as she scanned the rugged mountains to the east. So much for she and Bobby developing a friendship. Looked like he just remembered he didn't like her.

Twenty minutes later, Robert pulled over to the side of the road a few miles out of town. He looked across Bobby's head, weary lines prominent around his eyes.

Toni didn't even try to smile at him. What was the use?

"You can jog down to the bend in the road and back as many times as you like." He frowned. "But don't turn the corner. Understand?"

Without a word, she nodded and slid from the truck. Bobby didn't even bother to look at her. Even when she'd gotten out at home to change clothes he hadn't looked at her.

Sighing, Toni started out at a fast walk. Why did life have to be so complicated? Why couldn't her relationship with Robert be simple? Nothing had fallen into place, and it looked like it never would.

Picking up her pace to a slow, steady trot, thoughts of Robert and Bobby left her, and the shadow looming over her safety entered her mind. She breathed a tiny prayer, hoping for God's protection through the next few days— through today.

Toni inhaled, drinking the fragrance of fresh summer flowers, mountains, and trees. That man last night said he'd be back today to get her jewelry. Would she live to smell these mountains tomorrow?

With every step Toni took, her back protested where the gun had pressed. And that bruised spot was a steady reminder of the threat to her life. If he carried out the threat . . . She pushed the thought out of her mind.

180

Toni increased her jogging rate, matching her steady breathing pattern to the rhythm of her feet. She planned to run as long as her knee would let her. Slowly some of the tension slipped away, her headache dissipating.

A car approached from around the corner. Since Toni ran against the traffic, she eased to the side of the road and onto the grass, leaving the lane clear. But she couldn't go too far. A twenty-foot drop gaped just beyond the narrow shoulder.

The white sedan came into sight. One tire left the paved highway and ran onto the gravelly shoulder. Frowning, Toni trotted further away from the road, glancing cautiously toward the gully. The car slowed, and Toni realized she'd jogged past the road's bend. So she turned around, planning to cross to the other side of the road after the car passed.

The sedan neared, and several pieces of gravel flew up, stinging her legs. The radiator's heat engulfed her as the engine roared closer.

Scowling, Toni craned her neck, glancing over her shoulder. The white car gained speed from only a few feet away and headed toward her. Its radiator loomed behind like a monster's teeth.

Toni's heart pounded as she recalled the same scene two years ago. Turning her head, she stretched forward, extending her legs as fast and far in front of her as her height allowed.

The car sped up, her ears roaring with the engine's vibration. Toni's stomach churned in hot terror. He was close, and in only a matter of seconds . . .

She ran harder, pumping her arms up and down. But Toni's right foot slid out of control along the loose dirt and gravel at the gully's edge.

Gasping, she jerked toward the road, trying to regain her balance. The car rushed closer. Toni teetered on the precipice, feeling as if she were about to fall into eternity.

Inhaling, she blinked and swallowed convulsively, her arms and legs shaking out of control. Her right foot lost what little hold it had on the loose dirt and hung in midair. The gully's rocky bottom glared up at her, beckoning her downward.

Flailing her arms in desperation, a dry sob tore from Toni's gut. But the gully won, pulling her into its waiting arms.

Her intestines crashed against her abdominal wall as she fell to the jagged boulders beckoning below. The ground reached out, slamming against her body. An excruciating pain screamed from her skull.

Tires grated against gravel. And darkness closed in. . . .

CHAPTER 23

Gripping the leather-covered steering wheel, Robert frowned. He told her not to run around the corner. And she'd done it anyway. Stubborn female. He cranked the truck.

"Where'd she go?" Bobby asked, pulling his gaze from a squirrel in a tree to the road.

"She ran around the corner," Robert growled.

A white car roared toward them, careening down the other side of the road at breakneck speed.

Robert scowled as uneasiness gripped his heart. Driving to the road's curve, he strained for a glimpse of Toni's pink T-shirt. No Toni. The uneasiness grew to panic, his palms moistening the steering wheel. He licked his lips and accelerated around the next curve. Still no Toni.

Robert's chest tightened into a ball of screaming nerves. He gripped the steering wheel and did a U-turn in the middle of the road. "Hold on, Champ."

Leaning forward, Bobby peered out the windshield. "What do you think happened?"

Robert glanced at Bobby and slammed on the brakes. "I don't know. I hope that car didn't . . ." Robert crammed the truck into park and jumped from it. "Toni! Toni!" he yelled.

Bobby ran up beside him. Robert grabbed his arm. "Go that way." He pointed to the left. "See if you can see any sign of her."

Robert's face beaded in perspiration, his muscles tensing as he ran up the road. "Toni!" *Dear Lord, if she's . . . Please don't let her be . . . Oh God, I love her too much for . . .* "Toni!"

Robert scanned the road, the trees, the pasture not far away, hoping she'd step from behind a tree, wearing that heavenly smile.

"Dad! Dad!" Bobby scrambled from the side of the road, and ran toward him. "I think I found her!"

A thrill shot through Robert's midsection. He rushed for Bobby who met him halfway. Grabbing Robert's arm, he ran to the gully's ledge.

Bobby dropped to his knees. "Listen, you can hear somebody moanin' down there."

Robert squatted beside Bobby, grabbed the gully's edge, and leaned out as far as he dared. Holding his breath, he glimpsed a patch of pink through the shrubs lining the rocky wall. A pain-filled groan rose to him. "Toni!"

"Robert?" she croaked.

"Thank You, God," he breathed, his heart pulsating in warm relief. "I'm comin' down. Don't move."

He scanned the road both ways. To the right, the decline wasn't as steep. Robert grabbed Bobby's arm. "Stay here and keep talkin' to her."

Robert ran up the road and rushed into the gully. Fighting weeds and rocks, he stumbled down the side of it. Toni's low groans guided him in the right direction.

She might be alive, but that didn't mean she wasn't injured—possibly severely. What if her neck or back were broken? Robert gritted his teeth and ran. Bobby's voice floated down to him.

The weeds got thinner. The rocks took over. Robert clawed at the rocky side for balance. She couldn't be much farther.

He saw her white running shoes and rushed forward. "Toni!"

Her legs sprawled across the loose rocks, her hair matting to her face in a dirt-blood mixture. And her left arm lay at an odd angle.

Robert dropped beside her, blinking his stinging eyes. "Where do you hurt?"

"All over," she whispered. "He tried to run over me." Her eyes slid shut.

Robert touched her cheek, not daring to move her. Toni's face was scratched, her arms full of abrasions. Robert gulped for air. "Please don't die. . . ."

One hour later, Robert paced back and forth in the hospital's emergency waiting area. He felt as if his whole world balanced on what the next few hours held.

Bobby sat in a cushioned chair, fidgeting with nothing. "Do you think she'll be okay, Dad?" he asked for the sixth time.

Robert sank down beside him, patting his hand. "I hope so."

"I . . . don't guess I was too nice to her, was I?"

Robert smiled, patting his son's shoulder. "Don't you worry about that—"

"I mean . . . I just wondered if it was my fault that . . . " He inhaled. "I mean since I was so mean. . . ." He looked up at Robert, anxiety marring his dark eyes.

"No, Bobby," Robert said in surprise. "What happened

185

today had nothing to do with you." He gripped Bobby's shoulder in reassurance.

Bobby nodded his head and stared at the pay phone as if his mind were full of more than Robert knew. Robert wondered exactly what all Bobby had done. He and Toni had been discussing something hot and heavy when Robert had come back into the clinic's waiting room earlier today. If Toni lived, he'd find out. Robert blinked. He couldn't think like that. She was going to live. And that was final!

The emergency room door flew open. "Have you heard anything?" Dr. Weston asked. Marge gripped his hand and looked at Robert anxiously.

"No." Robert checked his watch. "She's in X-ray now."

"Do you know what happened?" Marge asked.

Robert rubbed his forehead. "All she said before she blacked out was, 'He tried to run over me.' That's all I know." Gritting his teeth, Robert slammed his fist against the chair arm. "It's my fault. I should've never let her run."

Marge sat beside him. "You can't blame yourself," she said, laying a hand on his arm. "I didn't try to stop her either. How could we have known?"

"Did you see the car?" Dr. Weston asked.

Robert nodded. "Yeah. It was a white Chevrolet. Early eighties model, I'd say. Colorado license. But I didn't get the number. He was going too fast."

Dr. Weston sat beside Bobby. "I wonder if it was the same person who ran over her two years ago."

Robert tugged his mustache in frustration. "I don't know." Sheriff Braxton still hadn't found Derek, and Robert was beginning to wonder if they'd been wrong in their assumptions. Murder number one fit Derek, but where was he? If he wasn't in Ouray how could he have been at Toni's house last night or even in that white car today? Derek was definitely up to something suspicious. Why else would he lie about not being able to swim? Maybe he was in cahoots with somebody. But who? Perhaps the make of the car would give them enough evidence to nail whoever was behind this.

"You found her in that gully?" Dr. Weston asked.

"Well, Bobby's the one who found her." Robert smiled at his son with pride. "All I can figure is she fell in the gully before the car got to her."

Marge shuddered. "That's about a twenty foot drop."

"I know," Robert said. Squeezing his eyes shut, he tried to blot the image of her limp body out of his mind.

The moments stretched by until a young doctor dressed in faded green scrubs strode toward them through a pair of swinging doors. "Are you with Toni Kirkpatrick?"

"Yes." Robert stood. He stopped breathing. This was it. *Please tell me she's going to live. Please tell me she isn't paralyzed.*

"Looks like Somebody was looking out for her. She's got a broken arm, some contusions, and by tomorrow she'll have her share of bruises, but that's extremely light compared to what it could have been."

The Westons sighed with relief.

Robert's hands shook, and he exhaled slowly. "May we see her?"

The doctor surveyed them all with dark eyes. "Are you Robert?"

Robert nodded.

"She keeps asking for you. I assume you're her husband?"

"I'm not, but—"

The doctor nodded in understanding. "Just one person right now. We're going to admit her for about thirty-six hours—give or take—for observation. She'll be in her room within an hour or so."

187

Dr. Weston laid his hand on Robert's shoulder. "We'll watch Bobby and call her parents."

Late that night Robert stood at the end of Toni's hospital bed and watched her sleep peacefully. The injection she'd received for pain had her out cold. Toni's golden-red hair sprawled across the pillow in silken softness. He'd spent the last twenty minutes gently brushing it and removing all the rocks and grass.

She'd rested throughout the evening, only stirring for water and a trip to the bathroom.

His heart swelled with love and thanksgiving that her injuries were slight compared to what they could have been. Turning, he gazed out the window to the lighted parking lot. A soft, steady rain pelted the window and trickled in tiny rivulets down the window pane.

Robert shut his eyes, letting the rain's rhythm wash over him, calming his tight nerves. He had so much to be thankful for. How many times lately had the woman he'd grown to love come through a bad situation alive?

Maybe God had protected her. It wasn't a coincidence.

The same God who had willingly forgiven Robert of everything—no questions asked. And the words that had recently engraved themselves in his mind echoed through the core of his being. *How can you hold a grudge against Wayne when God has forgiven you of so much?*

With his index finger, Robert traced the trail of a raindrop. He was tired. He was tired of wrestling against what he knew was right. He was tired of keeping the bitterness burning. He was tired of looking in the mirror and seeing a pair of eyes that got harder and harder every day.

Robert needed relief from this burden.

Yes. Wayne Freeman caused him a lot of pain. Wayne Freeman caused Bobby a lot of pain. But God could heal the wounds. And Robert wanted that healing.

188

"Father," he whispered, placing his hand against the cold glass as if he were reaching out to heaven. "Help me forgive Wayne. Help me to heal. It's been a rough, hard road. But I know this . . . this brick in my heart isn't what You want there. Give me the kind of forgiveness only You have."

A warm relief flooded Robert, and he knew God had heard his prayer. He knew the healing had begun.

Toni said it was sometimes a struggle to maintain the forgiveness, but Robert was ready to work through it. What Wayne did to him didn't take place overnight. And Robert knew that total healing wouldn't happen overnight either. But God would work in His own time.

Wayne Freeman may have torn up Robert's life once, but with God's help, Wayne wouldn't ruin the rest of it.

CHAPTER 24

Toni slowly opened her eyes and squinted against the sunlight squeezing through the blinds. There was an antiseptic smell. . . . Where was she? Why did she hurt all over? Her aching left arm protested as she tried to push herself up.

"Mornin'," a familiar voice said.

Toni opened her eyes wider and glanced around the room. Robert stood beside her bed. Bobby and her uncle and aunt hovered at the foot.

"Where am I?" she rubbed her dry tongue against the roof of her mouth.

"You're in the hospital," Robert said.

"Hospital?" Toni raised her head, but its throbbing forced her to relax against the pillow. She closed her eyes, and the memory of falling off the side of that gully flashed before her. Then she recalled Robert staying with her all evening. It was all coming back.

"I fell. . . . Did you catch him? The car—it was white."
Fear bombarded Toni's chest like war missiles. Someone
had tried to kill her. Was it the man who had broken in for
the jewelry?

"We're workin' on it," Robert said.

Toni's mouth felt like it was full of gauze bandages. "I
need water," she said, remembering strong hands supplying
water throughout the night.

Aunt Marge produced a glass of cool water. Toni drank it
greedily, letting its iciness wash away some of the fog in
her mind.

"How do you feel?" Robert asked, leaning over her.

Toni blinked up at him. His jaw and chin held what
looked like two days of stubble. Moving her usable arm
from under the covers, she touch his face. "You need to
shave."

Uncle Phil chuckled.

Robert's tired smile crinkled the corners of his eyes.
Clasping her hand next to his face, he turned it to kiss the
palm. "I think you're going to make it."

Toni nodded and smiled weakly. She moaned with pain.
"I hurt all over."

"Feel like eating something?" Uncle Phil asked. "You
slept through breakfast, but there's a fast food place close
by. I don't mind chasing down a sausage biscuit for you."

Toni's stomach growled with anticipation. "That sounds
good."

Uncle Phil headed for the door.

"Can you raise the head part of this bed a little, Robert?"
Her mind starting to clear, she observed Robert more closely than before. "You know, you really look beat."

Uncle Phil turned from the doorway and glanced at Toni.
"He wouldn't go home last night. Sheriff Braxton offered to
take over halfway through, but he wouldn't let him."

"It wouldn't have mattered if Sheriff Braxton had come

191

and planted himself and half the Durango police force outside that door, I wouldn't have budged," he said stubbornly.

He wore the same red plaid shirt and faded blue jeans he'd been in yesterday, along with the holstered pistol and shiny badge on his left shoulder.

"Besides, your mother kept calling," Robert said.

Uncle Phil snorted and walked out. "Lame excuse," Toni heard him say before the door closed behind him.

"Mother? Is she coming? There's no need—"

"No. I convinced her you were well looked after and are going to be perfectly fine. I told her everything, though."

"I got a phone call this morning from her," Marge said, looking at Robert. "She wanted to know who you were."

"I told her I was Toni's bodyguard."

"She didn't buy that."

"It's the truth."

"I know. But . . ." Marge trailed off, her dark eyes glistening.

Toni moved uncomfortably, knowing she'd be receiving a phone call, too. Mother had been humming the wedding march to Toni ever since she'd graduated from medical school.

She looked at Bobby who stared out the hospital window with his hands crammed into his jeans pocket. A scene flashed before her. She was lying in the gully, the rocks eating into her back, and she heard Bobby's voice calling for Robert. A streak of blind fear flowed through her. Who tried to run over her?

Toni blinked. "Bobby?"

He turned toward her.

"Thanks for finding me." She smiled, but not enough to hurt the cut on her right cheek.

Bobby smiled shyly, shrugged, and studied his sneakers.

Robert grasped Bobby's shoulder. "We're all proud of you."

"Ah, it wasn't nothin'," he mumbled.

"Well, I'm glad you were there," Toni said.

"Are you really?" Bobby asked, an inflection of faint surprise in his voice.

"Of course. Why shouldn't I be?"

"Well, I thought that since I—" He broke off, glancing around the room at all the grownups, his gaze landing on Toni.

Toni winked. "I'm very glad you were there."

"Bobby's staying to help me," Robert said as he re-entered the room. He'd walked out with the Westons as they left.

"Good," Toni said, smiling at Bobby.

Robert raised a black, leather case. "Your aunt and uncle brought my shaving gear and some fresh clothes. The nurses said they'd let me use an empty room to shower and shave. I'll just be two doors down, but Bobby's going to sit with you while I'm gone."

Toni swallowed and nodded as an evil, monster-like radiator flashed through her mind. Her heart kicked against her ribs. Would he try again?

Squeezing Toni's toes as he went by, Robert sauntered for the door. "Now y'all don't go conspiring against me again, you hear?"

"We won't," Bobby said, sinking into the chair next to Toni's bed as Robert left.

"I meant it when I said I appreciate your finding me," Toni said as soon as the door snapped shut.

Studying his fingernails, Bobby quirked his mouth. "Ah, Dad would've found you. He was runnin' around, screaming." He looked out the window.

"Well, I think you were great anyway." Toni gave Bobby the warmest smile she could conjure up and pushed the IV monitor back so she could see him better. "Do you like tacos?"

"Sure."

"Well, I owe you one. And when I get this cast off, I'm going to make you my own special gourmet tacos." She held her breath, wondering how Bobby would react. He'd almost forgotten he didn't like her yesterday at the clinic. Could he be changing his mind about her?

"That . . . sounds good," he said slowly. "I . . . I guess we . . . that is me and Dad could come over to . . . um, to eat 'em."

Toni shook her head. "Good then, it's a date." Wincing at her words, she prepared herself for Bobby's negative reaction.

But he sat quietly and studied her cast, his forehead creased. "I . . . um . . . Did you tell Dad about . . . about . . ." A red flush worked up his neck.

"About Tweety Bird?" she asked, knowing the incident must be heavy on Bobby's mind for him to inquire about it again.

"Yeah."

"No. I won't either—ever. And you can count on it."

"Thanks," he said, his forehead relaxing, the flush retreating. "I'm really sorry about . . . about that. It made me feel just awful. That's the . . . the worst thing I've ever done—ever. And then when . . . when that car . . . I thought you were . . . that the car had . . . that you were . . ."

"Dead?"

"Yeah. And boy, I felt somethin' awful."

Smiling, Toni watched two birds flit by her window. "You didn't have any reason to feel bad, Bobby. You'd already apologized."

"Yeah, but then you were nice to me about . . . about . . ."

"Tweety Bird?"

"Yeah." His apprehensive gaze held hers. "Then I . . . then I was mean in the truck again, and . . ."

"It's okay," Toni soothed. "Just forget it. It's all over. And

194

we're friends now. Right?" she asked, hoping he confirmed her declaration.

"Right," he said, tugging on the hem of his black T-shirt. Several minutes passed in which Bobby stared straight ahead as if he wanted to say more but didn't quite know how to say it. "Have you ever been married before?" he finally blurted.

Toni drew back in surprise. "No. Why?"

"My . . . my mom was killed in a car wreck when I was two. And I wondered if maybe the same thing might've happened to you—to your husband, I mean."

"No, I've never been married." Toni bit her bottom lip, trying not to smile.

Bobby rubbed his ear, looking like a miniature Robert. "I think Dad was right."

"About what?"

"He said you needed somebody to . . . to look out for you."

"Oh?"

"Yes. And he was right. You get into too much trouble to be by yourself."

"It's not like I tried to get into any of this. It just happened."

"I know. But still, I think he was right. And I think you need to do somethin' about it."

"Like what?"

"Well, have you ever thought about . . . about gettin' married?"

"What?" Toni sputtered, lifting her head. This nine-year-old boy was beginning to sound like Uncle Phil.

"Married. I think you should get married. Then maybe you won't get hurt any more." He pointed to her arm.

"Bobby, it isn't quite that easy."

"Why?"

"Well, nobody's asked me for starters." *Are we really hav-*

ing this conversation or is this a crazy dream? The pain in her left arm was real.

"Why don't you ask Dad? I know he'd say yes."

"What?" She stared at Bobby through widened eyes. "I can't ask your father to marry me. He . . . I . . ."

"Darla Mitchell asked me to sit by her on the last hay ride." He frowned. "I didn't 'cause I don't like girls. But there's not any difference in that and . . . and you askin' Dad."

"There's lots of difference!" Toni curled her toes. "Usually men do the asking when it comes to getting married. Besides, have you thought about the fact that if I marry your father, I'd be just as good as marrying you? I'd be right in the same house with you all the time."

"That's okay." Exhaling, he looked at the lavatory beside Toni's bed. "Dad's cookin' isn't as good as Mrs. Martin's and . . Can you cook?"

"Well, yes I . . . um . . . yes." Toni felt as if she were being interviewed for a job.

"Good. Sometimes Dad burns stuff."

"Oh?"

"So if . . . if Dad asks, will you?"

"What?"

"Marry him. If he asks, are you gonna marry him?"

"Bobby. . . ."

"We don't like microwave popcorn. But somebody's got to take care of you, or you're going to get killed. I thought . . . I thought when that car . . . I thought . . . you were dead." He looked at her with a concerned, dark gaze. "So if Dad asks, will you?"

Toni chuckled. "I . . . Bobby, he hasn't asked."

"Well I'll ask for him then. Will you marry us?"

"Us?"

"Yeah. Us."

Toni fidgeted with her sheets. She'd come a long way

with Bobby. Of course, if he hadn't stolen her bird and she hadn't almost been killed none of this would be happening. But still, Toni didn't want to hurt his feelings. Yet she couldn't say yes. "Bobby. . . ."

The door swished open, and Robert walked into the room. "All done," he said, rubbing his jaw. "Feels good too."

Toni sighed with relief.

"Did you keep a good eye on her while I was gone?"

"Yes sir. We talked." Bobby looked at Toni.

"Oh? What about?" Robert asked, laying his shaving kit and folded dirty clothes on the counter.

"I asked—"

"I could really use a glass of ice water," Toni said, throwing Bobby a pointed look.

"I'll get it," Robert said, glancing from Bobby to Toni. "Conspiring against me again, are we?"

"No," Toni said.

"Yes," Bobby said.

"No, we weren't," Toni said firmly, giving Bobby a look she hoped told him she'd gag him before she let him tell his father what they'd been talking about.

"I see," Robert said, handing Toni the glass of water. "You've got some explaining to do," he mumbled under his breath and glanced at Bobby.

Turning on the television, Robert found an old western and Bobby started watching it.

"I called the sheriff while I was out," he said in a lowered voice. "He said he found a wheel cover in the gully not far from where you went off the side. It says Chevrolet. That's what I thought it was. So we've got a solid lead."

Toni's throat tightened. "Do you think he'll find the car before I go back home?"

"I hope." He leaned toward her slightly and reduced his voice to a whisper. "And he found Derek."

Toni's eyes widened. "Where?"

"I . . . um . . ." Robert glanced at Bobby. "At the river near where I rescued Mr. Tankersly. He'd been beaten severely and left for dead. But he's still alive."

"Does the sheriff know if he's the one?"

Robert shook his head. "We don't know for sure. But things are startin' to look bad for him. He was lying beside a white Chevrolet."

"Where was his Mercedes?"

"The sheriff doesn't know yet."

"Does Sylvia?"

Robert shook his head. "We don't know. She isn't talking. They admitted him to the hospital in Grand Junction."

"Is he conscious now?" The knot in Toni's chest began to relax some. Was the nightmare finally over?

"He was unconscious, but Sheriff Braxton said he'd just called to check on him and they said he was coming 'round. He's going over there to question Derek. Whatever he's been playing at, his little game is over."

By five o'clock, the nurse had removed Toni's IV. Her doctor said she could go home, but Robert insisted she stay one more night. "Just to make sure everything's safe at home," he said. The doctor agreed, saying another night of hospital rest couldn't hurt.

Shortly after the doctor's exit, Heather Martin sailed through the doorway. Robert had arranged for her to pick up Bobby and keep him overnight.

"Well, good-bye," Bobby said, hovering uncertainly at Toni's side.

"Bye," Toni said, squeezing his arm.

Bobby crammed his hands into his jeans pockets and glanced over his shoulder at Robert, who was talking to Heather. "If he asks, are you going to?" he whispered.

Toni nodded. "If he asks . . ." She winked at Bobby, a

light happiness engulfing her. If Derek was the one who had tried to kill Mr. Tankersly, then her nightmare was over. And on top of that, Bobby was her friend.

"Toni," Robert said, approaching her bed. "Heather's having trouble with her car. It sounds to me like it's just a spark plug wire that's come undone. I'm going to run down and see if I can help her." He looked around the room as if he were hesitant to leave. "I don't think anything will go wrong. I was on the phone again with Sheriff Braxton a few minutes ago while the nurse was in, and it's looking like we've got our man. Sylvia just called him and said she's ready to talk." He paused. "That is . . . if nobody's involved in this with him, but . . ."

"Go on," Toni urged. "I'll be all right."

"I won't be gone but about fifteen or twenty minutes."

A few minutes after Heather and Robert left, Barbara Jones stepped in. With her arms wrapped around her, she looked cold even though she wore a blue sweater. Despite that, her eyes glowed with happiness, and her lips quivered into a smile. She ran a hand through her tousled hair. Walking further into the room, she glanced around.

"Daddy's lots better," she said in a soft, shaking whisper. "He's even starting to talk some."

"I knew our prayers would come through," Toni said. Looking up at Barbara, a warm glow invaded Toni's heart.

"Where's Robert?" Barbara asked.

"He just went down to help Heather Martin with her car. He should be back in about twenty minutes or so."

Barbara nodded. "There's something out in the hall I've got for you. I'll be right back." She turned and scurried out the door. And just as fast, she came back into Toni's room pushing a wheelchair.

Toni frowned in confusion. "What—"

"You're going for a little ride," Barbara said, the shaking gone from her voice.

199

Toni wrinkled her forehead. "But where? What—"

Barbara pulled a revolver from her sweater's pocket. "Get in this wheelchair. Now!" Her face twitched in agitation.

Toni's heart raced. "Barbara. . . ." She blinked. "It was you all the time?"

"Me? Oh no, honey." She yanked the covers off of Toni. "You're not going to play dumb with me."

"What?" The back of Toni's knees broke out in a clammy sweat against the cool sheet.

"He pays more attention to you than me, and I'm tired of it. Now he's going to prove he loves me and not you. I'm glad I didn't kill you when I ran you off the road yesterday. Now I'll get to watch him do it."

Toni's throat constricted in horror. "You ran me off the road?"

Barbara laughed. "You mean you didn't recognize his car?"

"Whose? Frank's?"

"You stupid, stupid little girl." Barbara grabbed Toni's right arm, forcing her aching body from the bed. "Maybe you really don't know what's going on here."

CHAPTER 25

Robert looked at Toni's rumpled sheets. She was gone. Blinking hard, he clenched his fists. Robert had looked up the hall and been to the nurses' desk, too. She couldn't have vanished. He'd only been gone ten minutes.

Inhaling, he tried to slow his heart rate. This couldn't be anything but a routine trip to X-ray or something the nurses had forgotten about, or—that didn't sound right. He wheeled around, ready to tear down the hospital brick by brick if he had to in order to find her.

A young, brunette nurse pushed open the door just as he was leaving. "Were you the one looking for Dr. Kirkpatrick?"

"Yes."

"I saw her going to visit a Mr. Tankersly on the fourth floor. She said he'd been one of her patients in Ouray. His daughter was taking her up there in a wheelchair."

201

Robert rubbed his ear and relaxed. "Did she say how long she'd be gone?"

The nurse shook her head. "But it shouldn't be too long."

Robert nodded. "Thanks."

Smiling, the nurse shut the door.

Robert stared at the bed. That was strange. Toni hadn't mentioned going to see Mr. Tankersly. A cold dread settled in his stomach like a lump of steel. He knew it must be leftover fear from all she'd been through. Surely Barbara wouldn't . . .

Robert pounded his left fist against his right palm. He had to find out what room Mr. Tankersly had been moved to.

Five minutes later, Robert tapped on Mr. Tankersly's door. Barbara opened it a few inches and peered out. Robert smiled, his tension easing some at the sight of how normal Barbara looked.

"Is Toni here?" Robert asked.

"Yes, she is," Barbara said, grinning. "Why don't you come in and visit, too?"

As Robert entered the room, someone clicked the door shut behind him. The smile disappeared from Barbara's face, and she pointed a small handgun at his gut.

Toni sat near the end of Mr. Tankersly's bed, strapped to a wheel chair. Her mouth was taped shut, yet her eyes spoke both terror and relief.

"Toni!" Robert looked from her to Barbara in confusion.

"That's right," a soft, male voice said from behind him. The man pushed the end of a gun against Robert's back.

Barbara moved to the head of her father's bed with her eyes narrowed and her gun leveled on Toni.

Robert's mind whirled as his heart pounded. So Barbara was at the bottom of this. But who stood behind him? "Barbara . . . if you dare. . . ."

"You're catching on real fast," the man said. "Now . . . let's see you lay your gun on the end of that bed nice and slow."

Robert hesitated.

"If you don't want the doctor with a hole in her head, do what he says," Barbara said.

Robert placed the gun on top of the white covers.

"Now walk over beside the doctor—slowly," Barbara said.

Robert walked forward, the gun still in his back.

Mr. Tankersly's gaze darted around the room. "Murder number one," he mumbled again and again.

"Shut up," Barbara said. "I'm sick of you, hanging on forever and ever, never dying. I'm sick of having to take care of you. I've paid my dues. Now I want my money."

Robert continued walking toward Toni. Every muscle in his body tensed, ready for attack. He couldn't, he wouldn't let these people get away with this. Licking his lips, he stopped beside Toni. Nobody, nobody tried to kill the woman he loved without a fight from him.

"You okay, Toni?" he asked. Placing a hand on her shoulder, Robert felt her shivering with fear.

Closing her eyes, Toni gave a shaking nod.

"Shut up," the gunman demanded, walking around Robert to face him.

Robert inhaled in surprise. He couldn't believe who was peering back at him.

"Don't look so shocked," the man said in a polite voice. "You've never heard of a woman deciding she picked the wrong brother?"

"Gordon? What—"

"Get away from her, Gordon" Barbara said, jealousy raging in her brown eyes.

Gordon moved beside Barbara.

"You two are having an affair," Robert said incredulously.

203

"That's right," Barbara said. "And it'll do the doctor good to remember that, too. Gordon is *my* man, and I'm sick of her having his attention all the time."

"What about Frank?" Robert asked, buying time. If he could get them talking, maybe . . .

"What about him?" Gordon replied.

"He's a jerk. He's mean. And I got sick of him," Barbara said.

"So you just changed brothers. Is that it?"

Barbara shrugged. "Sure."

"Murder number one. Murder number one," Mr. Tankersly whispered.

"I said shut up," Barbara said, slapping her father.

Robert winced, and the old man quieted. "Why does he keep saying that?"

"Between Doug and me, I'm the oldest," Barbara said in an uncaring voice. "The old man always called us Number One and Number Two when we were growing up."

Gordon gazed at Toni, a spark of twisted desire lighting his eyes. "Did you enjoy my visits as much as I did?"

Robert suppressed the urge to knock that smutty look off Gordon's face. "So, you're the one who stole Toni's jewelry?" he asked instead, trying to keep the disgust out of his voice.

"Yeah," he said, smiling wickedly.

"So that means you're the one who ran over her two years ago?"

"Yeah, it was me," Gordon said. "That was an accident. Too bad I didn't know the doctor then as well as I do now," he said, an intimate caress to his voice.

Swallowing, Robert balled his fists until his nails ate into his calloused palms.

"You're sorry . . ." Barbara glared at Gordon as if she were ready to shoot him along with Toni.

Shrugging, Gordon looked at her indifferently. "It was

your idea. You're the one who noticed she was wearing that diamond pendant at the hospital and figured she had more. And you're the one who said the jewelry would be enough to keep Doug happy till Tankersly died."

"Doug?" Robert asked.

"He's been blackmailing Gordon and me. He threatened to tell Frank unless we paid to keep him quiet. Then he just goes and gambles it all away," Barbara spit out. "He knew about Gordon running over Toni, too. And every time he ran short of cash, he swore he'd tell it all."

"People start knowing too much, and sometimes they show up dead," Gordon mused, pointing his gun at Robert, "like that stupid nurse."

"The nurse?" Robert asked, his mind reeling. Why did Gordon kill the nurse?

"Yeah, he was number two."

"And Mr. Tankersly was number one?"

"Oh, so you can count, too," Gordon said sarcastically. "And what comes after two?"

"Three . . . murder number three," Robert mumbled. So that's what he'd meant when he told Toni she'd be murder-number three.

"We've got plans to get rid of Doug and Frank, too, which is what we should've done a long time ago. That is of course, after we kill you." Gordon cocked his gun. "You shouldn't have come back from the parking lot so soon, cowboy."

"No!" Barbara said. "You're going to kill her first." She pointed at Toni. "And I'm going to watch you. I want her dead. And I want you to do it, you double-crossing—"

"I'm not killing her," Gordon said, turning on Barbara. "Maybe I'll kill you, and go to Europe with her instead."

Barbara's face ignited with fury. "You . . ." And she proceeded to call him every name Robert had heard, and some he hadn't.

Robert knew this was his chance. He jumped toward Gordon. His leg muscles sprang to life, his chest churning with adrenalin. Robert growled with anger as he delivered one kick to Gordon's wrist, sending the gun clattering toward the door, and a second kick to Gordon's stomach, causing the man to double in pain.

He turned to Barbara, ready to deliver the same treatment to her, but she cocked her gun and stared at him with cold, brown eyes.

"You make another move, and you're dead," she said in a controlled voice. The hatred pouring from her resembled the devil himself.

Robert stopped, his nerves tearing at his muscles like he'd crashed against a metal wall. Every beat of his heart erupted against his temples.

He breathed in short, fear-filled gasps, inhaling the smell of Toni's sporty perfume. "Okay, okay," he said softly as Gordon rolled on the floor and groaned. "I'm backin' up." *But not for long.*

A slow tear trickled down Mr. Tankersly's wrinkled face, a soft sob escaping him. Gordon gradually recovered and tried to stand. Robert couldn't let them get away with this.

The door swept open and someone walked in. "What's going on here?" Frank asked.

Barbara glanced toward the door.

Robert lunged forward, crashing the heel of his boot against Barbara's hand. The gun flew across the room, banging against the wall and falling to the floor.

Her face crinkled in surprised pain.

Robert scanned the floor. Spotting the gun, he dove for it. But so did Gordon. Robert landed on his knees, his hand closing over the gun the same time Gordon's did.

"Get my gun on the bed and the other one by the door," he yelled to Frank. "And call security!"

Hot flesh mingled with cold metal as Robert gritted his

teeth, determined to pry the gun from Gordon. Robert's arms ached as they wrestled across the floor. Gordon's finger reached the trigger. Robert struggled to break his iron grip as Gordon twisted to point the gun toward Toni.

"I'm going to kill her!" Gordon yelled. "If I can't have her, you can't either."

"Shoot her!" Barbara urged.

Sweat covered Robert, trickling down his back. Toni stared into the end of the gun and back to Robert in pale horror. Robert concentrated his strength to break Gordon's insane grip.

Gordon squeezed the trigger, and the bullet erupted from its chamber.

"No!" Robert screamed, stretching for Toni's wheelchair as the window exploded, sending a shower of glass slivers into the room.

"Security!" a man yelled from the open door.

Glancing at the three guards standing with drawn guns, Robert tingled with an onslaught of relief. "Toni?" he croaked.

She moaned through the tape over her mouth.

His eyes filled with tears, and he swallowed. "Toni."

CHAPTER 26

Four hours later, Toni raised her heavy lids to stare up into Robert's face. She smiled.

"How do you feel?" he asked, stroking her cheek.

She yawned. "Better. The pain medicine worked." With her right arm, Toni pushed herself up against her pillows, frowning as her legs and back protested.

Robert sank to the side of her bed. "Don't do too much. The doctor says you're to stay put." He took her hand in his, stroking the back with his thumb. "You scared me out of ten years of my life, Sunshine."

Toni shut her eyes and tried to convince her quaking heart the nightmare was over. "Did you get everything taken care of at the police station?"

"Yes. They'll want to question you tomorrow. But they're holding Barbara and Gordon."

"If Barbara didn't return my jewelry, who did?"

"Frank. The plumbing in Gordon's house had malfunctioned, and he was over there helping Gordon replace some carpet. He was looking in a closet and found it. He remembered seeing you wearing the unusual ruby cluster pendant once while you were visiting Mr. Tankersly and knew it was yours." Robert shrugged. "So he returned the jewelry."

"When you saw Barbara pulling out of your house, she was actually trying to break in and get it back, but she saw you coming. She'd gotten mad at Gordon about his distraction for you and stopped helping him after they put the snake in your house. But he forced her to go to your house and try to retrieve the jewelry. She'd seen Frank get into his car with the yellow pillowcase and drive toward your house. Anyway, Gordon said if she didn't he'd leave the country and call to turn her in."

"And Frank didn't suspect anything between Barbara and his brother?"

"He said he'd begun to suspect. That's why he was helping Gordon. It was an excuse to go through his house and see if he could find any proof. You know, some sign of Barbara having been with Gordon."

"Of the four of them, I would never have thought Barbara and Gordon . . . Doug and Frank, maybe, but—"

"I know. But being a jerk and disliking your father-in-law isn't against the law."

"He might only appear to be a jerk," Toni said. "I mean, a person who is honest enough to return my jewelry can't be a jerk through and through."

"I guess. Everybody's got their good quirks. Maybe Frank's just an honest jerk."

"Who can't stand his father-in-law."

"Yeah."

"What about Derek?"

"Derek's got his own problems." Robert inhaled. "Seems shortly after he moved here, he had a couple of visitors to

209

his hotel. He noticed the same two men checked in at regular intervals, stayed one night, and left town. After about a year of that, he got curious and bugged two rooms. The next time they came through, he assigned them the bugged rooms and listened. He learned they were launderin' money. So he—suggested—that if they didn't reward his silence, he wouldn't stay quiet."

"That's where his extra income came from."

"Right. But Derek was dealing with people bigger and meaner than he thought. They got tired of paying a small town hotel owner to keep quiet and decided to quiet him themselves. I think they really thought they'd killed him when they left him at the river.

"That's what he was really doin' at the river when he saw Mr. Tankersly. The men checked in and checked out without Derek ever acknowledging them. Then they met by the river once a month for Derek's payoff. He didn't go in after Mr. Tankersly because he'd just gotten a payoff and had the money on him. He didn't want to lose it in the river."

Robert brushed Toni's lips with a teasing kiss. "Barbara did tell the RN that Derek was Mr. Tankersly's grandson," he said against her ear then kissed it. "He did come to see Mr. Tankersly, just as he said."

Toni swallowed as flames shot down her neck and spread to her stomach.

"But Barbara lied to me to make Derek look guilty. She and Gordon knew we'd verify the stories with the RN."

"So they killed the nurse?" Toni asked, recoiling at the thought of such cold-bloodedness.

"Gordon killed him. He was murder number two." Robert pulled away from her and gazed into her eyes, a deep fire reflecting in his. "Barbara's the one who unplugged the ventilator. And they tried to kill Mr. Tankersly together. If you'll remember, Barbara said she was at home, but no one actually saw her."

"But . . . but Gordon had gone to Montrose," Toni stammered, unable to think straight or talk straight with him looking at her like that.

"Yeah. But he actually got back into town by eleven. He made sure Frank saw him leavin' at nine. Then after he'd finished his business, he snuck to Barbara's house, took care of Mr. Tankersly, threw him in the river, and made sure Frank saw him comin' back into town around one, like he'd just gotten back from Montrose."

"What . . . what about Sylvia? How . . . how'd she fit into all this?"

"She didn't, really. Her husband left her a fat life insurance policy. She invested well. It paid off."

"But I really thought she acted strange after my jewelry was stolen."

"She acted strange because she thought Derek had taken it. He'd borrowed her gun the evening before because he was going to demand more money from his source. Seemed he'd gotten himself in over his head with his new, extravagant lifestyle. That's why Sheriff Braxton found him by that white Chevrolet. His Mercedes had been repossessed, and he'd bought a used car."

Toni thought about Derek and Sylvia standing on Sylvia's porch and Derek mouthing "Don't worry," to her. "So she thought maybe he had burglarized my house?"

"Yes. As a matter of fact, she didn't tell him she thought that. She was afraid if he hadn't broken in and she acted like he had, Derek would get mad and break off the relationship again. But she got scared when Derek came up half-dead. So she called Sheriff Braxton, telling him she wanted to talk. I think she wanted some kind of protection for Derek, and she knew she could get it if she confessed for him."

"She must really care about him."

"She does. But he's broken her heart once, and I don't

think she's very sure of him."

"Why did he stop seeing her before?"

"Sheriff Braxton seems to think he got scared about gettin' too serious with a woman who had a ready-made family. He said he heard something like that when the breakup happened. Grapevine stuff."

Toni nodded. "I'm glad the whole thing's over. Now maybe I can get on with my life."

"Well, there's one other thing that's over. And I wanted you to know about it."

"What?"

Robert paused. "Last night, while you were restin', I asked God to help me with my problem with Wayne." He took a deep breath. "I know it's going to be hard. And I know all my feelings won't change overnight, but I'm willin' to give it a shot."

"That's all He asks," Toni said, placing her hand on his clean-shaven face. "I know I've forgotten that I've forgiven many times. And there've been a few times during all this when I thought I wouldn't be able to remember I had forgiven. But I can honestly say I have a deep peace within me and no hard feelings. I know you'll get there, too."

Robert nodded. "I . . . I don't think I can do it right now, but I think eventually I'd like to go see Wayne and tell him that I've forgiven him."

"That might mean more to him down the road than you'll ever know."

"I hope. We used to be best friends. Maybe . . ." He exhaled and looked at the ceiling. "It'll be hard."

"Yes," Toni said. "It won't be easy."

"I've also told Sheriff Braxton I'd go ahead and accept the deputy position on a full-time basis. I've got a few more jobs I've promised to finish. And after that, I'll be working with him."

"You going to run for sheriff?"

Robert shrugged and smiled. "Maybe. I know the race won't be easy, but—"

"Most things that are worthwhile aren't."

"Like us, Sunshine?" Robert touched her cheek.

Toni's pulse accelerated, and she noticed a flash of something in Robert's eyes she'd never seen before.

"I don't think I'd say what I'm about to say if I hadn't almost lost you. But . . . I love you, Toni. I think I was a goner the minute you asked me whether or not I was married when I brought that pie over."

Toni winced. "Was I that obvious?"

Laughter brimmed his eyes. "Very obvious."

Toni sobered. "I love you, too."

"And I think you should be warned. In two or three months, I might ask you to marry me."

"Bobby's already beat you to it."

"What?" Robert's eyes widened in surprise.

"Well, actually he said, 'Will you marry us?' "

"He asked you to marry us?"

"Yes. He came to the conclusion that I wasn't safe on my own. And at first he tried to get *me* to ask *you*."

"Maybe that's not a bad idea."

"We'll see," Toni said, smiling impishly. "But I have a rule. I never ask a man to marry me who doesn't keep his promises."

"What promise?"

"You promised me some wood. And you never brought it." Adjusting her cast, Toni looked at him in mock accusation.

Rubbing his right ear, Robert shrugged. "I forgot all about that wood. . . . But . . . um . . . maybe we'll be sharin' the same pile before much longer, and I won't have to worry about it," he teased.

"Maybe. Maybe not," Toni said. "Maybe Bobby and I will just team up and kick you out."

He laughed. "Believe me, you'd be asking for help before long. That boy can be as hardheaded as a mule."

"Oh well, he gets it honestly."

"Right," Robert said, rolling his eyes. "The thing I want to know is what you did to him to make him change his mind about you."

Toni looked at the potted fern her mother and father had sent. "Those files are top secret."

Robert turned her chin, forcing her gaze to meet his. He narrowed his eyes. "Why do I get the feelin' this has something to do with Tweety Bird?"

Toni shrugged. "I don't know why you have that feeling." She made every effort to sound innocent, but knew she sounded completely guilty. Yet it was the truth. She didn't know why Robert had that feeling.

"Toni, you aren't keeping something from me that I, as a parent, should know, are you?"

Toni swallowed, torn between her promise to Bobby and loyalty to Robert. "Okay, I'll tell you the whole story."

"That sounds better."

"And I'll do it at Bobby's high school graduation. That is, if I'm still around, and he doesn't object."

"Toni!" Robert growled and then laughed, kissing her nose. "Whose side are you on, anyway?"

"I'm on my side, and so is Bobby. If I were you, I'd just let well enough alone."

"I will . . . until his graduation. And don't think I'll forget either, because you will be around."

"You sound very sure of yourself."

"I meant it when I told you I'm going to ask you to marry me. But I want to give you time to think. I don't want to rush this."

"Well, for your information if you just happened to ask in a few months, I might just happen to say yes. So you better be sure."

214

"Oh, I've never been more sure of anything in my life," he said against her lips.

A few minutes later he lifted his head.

"Robert?" Toni whispered weakly.

"Yes?"

"I just hate laundry."

He chuckled. "I hate microwave popcorn."

"If I eat my popcorn outside, will you do your own laundry?"

"It's a deal."